D1431468

SCANDAL IN BABYLON

SCANDAL IN BABYLON

Barbara Hambly

SEVERN HOUSE

First world edition published in Great Britain and the USA in 2021
by Severn House, an imprint of Canongate Books Ltd,
14 High Street, Edinburgh EH1 1TE.

Trade paperback edition first published in Great Britain and the USA in 2022
by Severn House, an imprint of Canongate Books Ltd.

severnhouse.com

British Library Cataloguing-in-Publication Data
A CIP catalogue record for this title is available from the British Library.

ISBN-13: 978-0-7278-9038-2 (cased)
ISBN-13: 978-1-78029-808-5 (trade paper)
ISBN-13: 978-1-4483-0546-9 (e-book)

All Severn House titles are printed on acid-free paper.

Typeset by Palimpsest Book Production Ltd.,
Falkirk, Stirlingshire, Scotland.
Printed and bound in Great Britain by
TJ Books, Padstow, Cornwall.

For Laurie

ONE

He swept her into powerful arms, pressed his lips to hers. The dark-haired woman gasped, struggled to turn her face aside, and the moonlight glimmered on the jewels that circled her throat, and gleamed on the half-unveiled marble of her breasts. Her small hands thrust at his mighty shoulders, clawed at the velvet of his cloak. But even as she struggled, her efforts melted into the grip of passion. The face she tried vainly to avert turned back, as if against her will, and her dark eyes closed with her surrender to passion and destiny . . .

'*CUT!*' Madge Burdon snatched off her plaid cap and hurled it to the studio floor. '*Beautiful!* Only, Kitty, if you could turn your head back and forth a little more. You're really in love with this man, even though you hate him. And when Dirk grabs you tighter, really *melt* into his arms—'

'If Dirk grabs my butt again,' announced Kitty Flint – known to film fans from Jersey City to Yokohama as the incomparable Camille de la Rose – in her breathless little-girl coo, 'he's gonna get a knee in the balls and then we'll *really* see somebody melt. Do you have any gin, darling?' She turned those immense brown eyes, fringed with lashes like enameled black wire, toward her sister-in-law.

'No gin.' Emma Blackstone stepped over the stretched line of string that demarcated the camera area, lipstick and mirror in hand. After nearly six months in Hollywood she still felt rather like Alice stepping through the looking glass, tall and prosaic and a little gawky in her Oxford tweeds among the shadowy splendor of moonlight in Babylon . . .

Not that the moonlight was real. Nor, indeed, had Babylon been anything more than a heap of ruins when Roman centurions like Marcus Maximus (alias Dirk Silver) were attempting to seduce its empress in (supposedly) the first century AD . . .

But . . . *διό καί φιλοσοφώτερον καί σρου δαιότερον ποίησις ἱστορίας ἐστίν*, Aristotle had remarked – Emma could still hear Professor Etheridge at Somerville College intoning the ancient sage's wisdom from on high. *Poetry is something more philosophical and more worthy of serious attention than history.*

Frank Pugh, studio chief and part-owner of Foremost Productions, would doubtless agree, though probably not in those words.

That was always supposing one could consider the scenario of *Temptress of Babylon* 'poetry'.

'Nertz.' Kitty sighed, took the lipstick, and set about repairing the ravages that passion and destiny had wrought on her make-up. The kleig lights snapped off, and without their greenish-blue glare the Motion Picture Yellow of the rest of her face looked garish, without in the least, Emma reflected admiringly, impairing the beauty of those delicate features.

'Just as well.' The Empress of Babylon shrugged her perfect (and largely uncovered) shoulders. 'I've simply *got* to find a new bootlegger before this weekend. I swear that last shipment of gin was straight out of his brother-in-law's bathtub.' She pursed her lovely mouth first into a pout, then into a kiss as she renewed its crimson gloss. A yard away, old Herr Volmort from Make-Up, looking more than ever like a bleached lizard in the rather grimy glow of the working lights, assisted Dirk Silver in the same task. Emma wondered what actual Babylonian empresses would have used to embellish their charms – the recipes for cosmetics she had encountered in Ovid and Juvenal didn't sound like anything she'd want on her own face.

Well, she could use wine-lees, I suppose . . . But where would one get wine-lees in the United States these days, given the existence of Prohibition?

'And I swear Dirk waxes his mustache with motor-oil.' Kitty handed the lipstick back to her. 'Thank you, sweetheart. Would you be a darling and see if you can find me something decent to drink in my dressing room?'

In six years of date-categorizing Roman statuary – both in her Oxford studies and as her archaeologist father's assist-ant – Emma had never encountered anything resembling the debonair, pencil-thin adornment of the leading man's upper lip. Or would Aristotle (or Professor Etheridge) consider that disregard of fact as another demonstration of the work's Moral Purpose?

She stepped back over the string that divided the moonlit night in Babylon from the reality (*if such it can be termed . . .*) of Stage One at one thirty in the afternoon, and behind her Miss Burdon bellowed, '*Lights!*' in a baritone that would have shaken the foundations of Olympus. '*Camera! Action!*'

Emma collected an astrology magazine from the nearest folding-chair (*Daily Guide to Finding Your Man!*), and watched as Kitty moved back toward Dirk. Arms extended, dark eyes – as the script instructed – 'incandescent with hatred, dread, and passionate desire' she bore a marked resemblance to a woman confronting a tarantula on the bathroom wall. For all her breathtaking beauty, Kitty was one of the worst actresses Emma had ever seen.

Dirk's lips descended upon those of the beauty palpitating in his arms. But as he crushed her to his armored bosom she suddenly pushed him away in mid-palpitation . . . 'Oh, Emma, darling, I almost forgot!' ('*Cut!*' roared Miss Burdon.) Kitty fished in the abbreviated gauze recesses of her costume and produced an envelope. Emma would have bet her next week's tea-money that the garment could not have concealed as much as a postage stamp.

'This came for you, and Fishy' – Conrad Fishbein was the head of Foremost Productions' publicity department – 'had it sent to my dressing room.'

Mrs Emma Blackstone, it said. *C/o Foremost Productions, Hollywood, USA.*

The sight of the handwriting was almost a physical shock. Emma turned her face quickly aside, trying to remember, as tears closed her throat, how long it had been since she'd actually cried.

Mother . . .

It wasn't actually her mother's hand. She knew that. Aunt Estelle's writing was the same as Mother's . . . Both had attended The Misses Gibbs' Select Academy for Young Ladies back home, and had had that copperplate perfection sharply smacked into them with an oaken ruler. As had Emma, in her turn. She looked again and yes, through the blur of tears she saw the Calcutta postmark.

Definitely Aunt Estelle.

She had the envelope open before she reached the little encampment that Kitty always had set up for herself in the corner of any studio 'stage', and the scent of her aunt's dusting-powder sliced her heart like broken glass. Guerlain's sandalwood with its touch of vanilla. Her mother had used the same. The memory of comfort mingled with bottomless grief, as if her parents had died last week instead of four years ago.

'*Lights!*' boomed Madge Burdon. '*Camera!*'

Emma lowered the letter, and looked around among the collapsible tables and make-up kits for a handkerchief. Hollywood was not a place for genuine tears.

Kitty had a dressing room, of course. It was fancier – and larger – than the parlor of The Myrtles, Emma's home back in Oxford . . . or what had been her home. But in Kitty's opinion it was too far from the shooting-stage – about a hundred feet – and there were absolute necessities in Kitty's life that had to be instantly on hand: two canvas folding-chairs, an emergency make-up kit, a thermos-bottle of coffee, three mirrors, a silver vase containing three dozen blood-red roses from an admirer, two of Kitty's kimonos ('I don't know what costume I'm going to be wearing, darling, and the red one doesn't go with everything . . .'), a gramophone and a half-dozen recordings, a porcelain vase containing pink lilies from another admirer, extra stockings, five silk pillows, a manicure set, a small pile of fan-letters, two astrology magazines and three Pekinese wearing diamond-studded collars.

('*Darling*, this is *nothing!*' had protested Kitty, in response to Emma's startled expression the first day Emma had accompanied her to the set. Emma had later discovered the truth of that statement.)

Frank Pugh considered nothing too fine for his best-known and most wildly popular star.

After six months here, Emma still felt as if she had been dropped on another world. Barsoom, perhaps. Or Oz.

Plumeria Lodge, Calcutta
March 14, 1924

My dearest Emma,
  Please, I beg of you, forgive me for not writing you before this. I had no idea of your situation – I had somehow formed the notion that following the death of your parents you had gone to live with your father's cousin Arminta and her husband in Leeds. But a mutual friend, recently married to a supervisor on the Grand Trunk Railway, informed me only this week that following your parents' decease (and I do not know if you even received my letter at the time. The influenza was so bad here – millions dead – that services were much disrupted) you were reduced to the position of PAID COMPANION, first to some vulgar button-manufacturer's widow in Manchester, and then to an AMERICAN ACTRESS (if one can use such a term of a CINEMA PERFORMER).
  I understand, from enquiries, that this woman is employed at Foremost Productions, a film studio in Hollywood, California, and I pray that this letter will reach you.

'*Music!*' roared Madge, and slashed a hand at the on-set musicians, who dropped straight back into the overture from *Swan Lake* on the very note they'd left off five minutes before. The kleigs went up with a blinding glare. '*Camera! Action!*'
  Incandescent with hatred, dread, and passionate desire, the Empress Valerna (*Valerna is NOT a Babylonian name!* Emma had objected, to no avail, when handed the scenario to 'doctor' six weeks ago . . .) swiveled her head back and forth like a clockwork doll, as Marcus Maximus enfolded her yet once more in muscular arms.

  Your uncle David and I are leaving at the end of the week on the *Empress of Jakarta*, bound first for Hong Kong and then for Honolulu and Los Angeles. We reach New York and board the *Ravenna* for Southampton on May 10th. We are scheduled to arrive in Los Angeles (or

San Pedro, which I am given to understand is nearly the same thing) on the 30th of April.

Please wire us IMMEDIATELY if you receive this message. Now that David's term with the Calcutta office is done we will be taking a house in Oxford again, and that home will be yours as well. Brian is in his last term at Queens, and Cynthia, who is quite a grown-up young lady now, will be returning to us also – so strange to be living under the same roof as one's children again, after all those years of letters from boarding schools! (Though of course Bella remains at the Roedean School and Lawrence continues at Eton.) We will be staying at the Peak Hotel in Hong Kong, and the Halekulani Hotel (I believe this is how it is spelt) in Honolulu.

'*Fantastic!*' The director hurled her cap to the floor again in her ecstasy. 'That was amazing! Print that one . . . Make a note, Zal—'

Cameraman Zal Rokatansky was already doing so in his notebook.

'*A house in Oxford.*' Emma tasted the words and felt tears flood her eyes again. '*A house in Oxford.*'

Fog veiling the willows on the Cherwell. People who understood when you made a joke about Aristotle. Tea with the Dean of New College and the solid joy of seeing a passage in one of Horace's *Odes* suddenly make sense of details noted in a Pompeian fresco. Secret gates to secret gardens of quiet colleges . . .

The world she had lost.

The person she had been.

'*That home will be yours as well . . .*'

The world that had been taken from her. Not just Jim – Emma understood that soldiers died in war, even soldiers deeply loved by the women to whom they'd only been married for six weeks. Her brother Miles had already been dead when the influenza came, a year after that. A mercy, given the little of him that had survived to be sent home like a blind and voiceless parcel. Even that loss, she'd understood, and had been prepared for. *Vitaque mancipio nulli datur*, Lucretius had written. *Life is given to no one for a lasting possession.*

But somehow she had never thought that it would be her mother and her father both. And not so soon after Jim and Miles. It had never even occurred to her that The Myrtles would be sold, mortgaged to cover poor Miles's medical bills. That she would be without a home, as well as without family, when she herself came out of hospital. Her father's whole income had derived from investments in Russia and Germany. Opening her eyes after that week of delirium, it had been like waking after a shipwreck, to find herself, like Viola in *Twelfth Night*, cast up on the shores of a foreign land.

The house had already been sold by that time. In the years she'd spent as a paid companion to Mrs Pendergast in Manchester (and 'vulgar' did not even approach the actuality of the woman) Emma had sometimes wondered who had bought The Myrtles. Who was sleeping in the room where she'd slept. But she'd never had the courage (or the time . . . or the train-fare . . .) to go and find out.

She had not been back to Oxford at all.

Now it was all being offered back to her, like a door opening in what had seemed to her a blank and barren wall.

'Kill the lights!' yelled Madge. 'Ned, you got everything ready out back for the elephant scene? Torley's gonna have that baby here at two and it's quarter after one now. Where the hell is Darlene?'

Dear child, I cannot express to you my feelings at not having made inquiries before this, nor to have made sure that you were safe. Everything that your uncle and I can do to make it up to you – to give you a decent home and a decent chance at life again – be sure that we will do.

Please believe me to be,

Your affectionate,

Aunt Estelle

Emma closed her eyes.

Oxford.

I can go home.

'Everything OK?'

Zal Rokatansky stood beside her. Medium height – and still
three inches shorter than Emma's five-foot-ten-inch gawkiness
– with his close-clipped, rust-colored beard and his cap turned
backwards to stay out of the way of the camera, he had his
usual aspect of a bespectacled teddy bear.

Going home will mean leaving Zal.

She didn't know what to do with that thought. 'Yes, everything's all right.' She quickly wiped her eyes, folded the letter
and tucked it into its envelope. 'From my mother's sister. The
only one left of my family, who didn't die of the influenza.'

By the tilt of his head, he clearly saw there was something
she wasn't saying. But before she could make up her mind
what to say at this point – if anything – Emma's thoughts
were interrupted, as they so often were in Hollywood, by
Madge yelling, 'Duchess! You following that? You're gonna
have to rewrite scenes twenty to twenty-four. We're three days
behind schedule and we can catch up if we dump all that
horseshit about the fortune teller—'

At the same moment Kitty squeaked, 'Darlings!' and floated
towards the encampment of make-up tables and Pekinese with
her ivory arms thrown wide. 'Did Mama's celestial creamcakes miss her?' The imperial harlot who in scene fifty-six
would send a hundred innocent Christians to martyrdom in
Rome's arena fell to her knees and embraced her fluffy pets
like a child. Chang Ming and Black Jasmine yanked on their
leashes and threshed their plumed tails in ecstasy. Buttercreme,
as usual, hid in her wicker carry-box, her invariable reaction
to being taken to the studio or in fact anyplace at all. 'Oh, my
little sweetnesses . . .'

'And where the hell is Darlene? We can shoot scene fifteen
before the elephant gets here—'

'I'm sorry.' Emma turned quietly to Zal. 'Why do we need
to dispose of the soothsayer? Without that foreshadowing . . .'

'Mostly because Gully Ackroyd's on a bender again,' said
Zal. 'And Frank doesn't want to replace him or reshoot. I'll
fill you in over coffee, if you're up to an epic saga.'

'It can't be any worse than the *Aeneid.' Or for that matter,*
she reflected, *Temptress of Babylon . . .*

Four months previously, while accompanying Kitty to a location shoot in the wilds of the California desert (and no advert she had ever seen had so much as hinted that nearly a quarter of California was a desert), Emma had been press-ganged into an emergency job of hastily rewriting a scenario (*Royal Desire*) based extremely loosely upon the Book of Esther. ('Emma knows *all* about all that ancient stuff!' Kitty had touted her proudly.) So effectively had she accounted for the unscheduled exchange of one leading man for another ('You know how much reshoots *cost?*' had roared Mr Pugh in dismay) that in addition to her original chores of brushing the dogs, balancing Kitty's checking account, and locating stray earrings, she had been given scenarios to rewrite, should Dirk or Nick Thaxter (playing Nero to Kitty's Babylonian Temptress) or Darlene Golden (the ethereal and perennially unclothed Christian heroine) feel their own acting talents were being unfairly scanted.

At the moment – Foremost Productions' regular scenarist being swamped with rush-jobs for three other projects – there was talk of Emma being given the entire scenario for Kitty's next film: story, action, and dialog cards.

The title of this opus was *Hot Potato*, so Emma was fairly certain that her scholarly father would turn over in his grave.

'And for Chrissake,' added Madge, 'who let *her* in here? *Bud!*' she roared, as the queenly form of gossip columnist Thelma Turnbit materialized from the shadows. '*Ned!* Somebody kick her out—!'

As the journalist extended an arm to catch Dirk Silver by the elbow, Kitty rose with the fluid grace of a dancer and intercepted her, purring, 'Thelma, *darling!*' Her natural baby-coo transmuted seamlessly to the smoky purr of a man-eater who had, over the past four years, devoured the hearts of two dozen cinematic fools for breakfast. She slipped an arm through that of Mrs Turnbit, and turned her radiant smile upon the approaching guard and the prop man's assistant. 'We won't be but a minute.' Her gesture of thanks towards the director was a miniature miracle of gratitude and stubbornness, before she turned to her sister-in-law. 'Emma, darling, might I trouble you to bring tea for myself and my friend here? The lights, you know,' she sighed to Mrs Turnbit, and put the backs of her knuckles lightly to her brow. 'One finds oneself in need of something . . .'

'Something', in Kitty's case, usually meant 'gin', but nobody was about to say so in the presence of this representative of *Screen Stories*. Particularly not now, when the talk of Hollywood was a contest in print for 'Who Is The Goddess of the Silver Screen?' The weird blue-white glare of the lights snapped off once more. The huge rear doors of Stage One were thrown open, and Herr Volmort scuttled to overtake Marcus Maximus with powder-puff and tubes of Motion Picture Orange and lipstick of a shade judged to be both cinematic and manly.

Madge looked on the point of protesting that they were three days behind and scene fifteen could be shot in just a jiffy, but Zal stepped across to the fuming director: 'I think Pugh'll want this one to pass, Madge. If Kitty gets voted Goddess of the Silver Screen – the Gal with "It" – it'll mean killer box office for the picture.'

Madge's mouth closed. In addition to being the producer of *Temptress of Babylon* and part-owner of Foremost Productions, Frank Pugh was The Man – so far as he knew, anyway – in Kitty's life.

During this whole interchange, Doc Larousse and his electrical crew were breaking down the lights, and Ned Bergen's myrmidons were moving crocodile-legged divans and portable gardens of potted fern out through the rear doors and into the garden set just beyond. When Emma had arrived with Kitty at six that morning, the prop chief had been in the midst of dressing the garden set, and now, through the doors, Emma could see pasteboard archways, potted palms, and a veritable army of semi-nude statues of heroes and gods in the clear California daylight.

'Somebody tell Darlene to get her ass in here,' shouted the director, pausing in the wake of the caravan. 'Where's the frikkin' guards? And somebody round up those goddam slave-boys!'

Zal joined Emma beside the trestle table at the other end of the barn-like 'stage', where the plebeian thermos bottles of the crew stood ranked. Given the fact that Kitty's coffee thermos was liberally spiked with bootleg rum, Emma guessed that it was her own ration of tea that was being generously offered to the guest.

'What is "It" anyway?' she asked, as the cameraman poured some of his own coffee into one commissary cup and started examining the others in quest of two that were clean. 'If Kitty is supposed to have it . . . I asked her and she defined it as "Oomph" . . .'

'"*It*"' – the cameraman held up a pedagogical forefinger – 'is defined as the human characteristic that draws all others with magnetic force. At least that's what Elinor Glyn says.'

'Mrs Glyn the novelist?' Emma had met her compatriot at the studio Christmas Party – like a film vamp herself in veils, jet beads, and feathers – and had enjoyed her views on cats, Prohibition, screen-writing, and American cooking.

'That's the one. She came up with it, you know, I forget in which book.' His voice shifted into the breathy register of passion. '"*With 'It' you win all men if you are a woman – and all women if you are a man . . .*"'

'And here I thought that was the definition of money.' Their fingers touched on the cup's fat porcelain handle and she smiled. '*Pecuniate obediunt omnia*, my father would say. "All things obey money".'

'Sounds like you've been in Hollywood too long.' Zal returned her smile. 'What would Dad have said "It" was for a woman?'

'*Quod nominatur non potest* . . . "That which is not to be named." At least not in polite circles.' She could almost hear him say it. Almost see the donnish twinkle in his eyes. And then, to cover the pinch of grief in her heart, she added, 'Myself, I should say that "It" would signify a good lighting-man.'

He laughed, found another clean cup, and sacrificed one of his store of clean spare handkerchiefs – he carried half a dozen for keeping his camera lenses spotless – to polishing it before he gave it to her. 'And remind me to go through the garden out there and get these back before we shoot, would you? Every extra on the lot has been sitting out there all morning, and we can't let the audience go around thinking the empress had a cup of joe while sitting on her throne.'

'I'm sure half of them think it anyway,' pointed out Emma. 'Kitty certainly does. And my father would have said that it was no more than could be expected, of Hollywood.'

'If that was your father's only complaint about the picture, he wasn't paying attention.' Zal looked for a moment as if he was about to ask her something else – as if he guessed that there was something about that letter that troubled her – but turned instead and went to gather up his precious Bell and Howell on its spindly legs, to carry outside. Emma lost sight of him among a knot of Roman soldiers and a platoon of muscular young Nubians recruited from the jazz clubs along Central Avenue, all clothed in gaudy loincloths and bearing long-handled, ostrich-plume fans.

No more than could be expected of Hollywood. Her throat tightened again as she tidied cups, sugar, cream and her thermos onto a tray, exactly as her governess had shown her, back in a world as far distant from her, now, as the sunlit Roman garden visible beyond the great doors.

At this moment in England it was damply cold and the first anemic baby leaves were barely dusting the April trees.

Doc Larousse and his crew wore short-sleeved cotton shirts, and sweat glistened on their faces and arms. Floyd at the front gate had assured her that warm spells like this week's happened every April: 'It'll be all gray and gloomy again in May.'

No wonder people in Los Angeles all run about half-dressed.

'I do not understand,' Kitty was saying, her great brown eyes soulful as Emma bore her tray back to the encampment, 'these women – these actresses – who put on one self before the cameras, and make themselves someone else, like *that*' – she snapped her delicate fingers – 'for other people they are with. I am as I always have been. I cannot help it.'

She sighed deeply, and cast down her gaze, as if she had never in her life danced the Charleston on a tabletop at the Coconut Grove or dared Doug Fairbanks to demonstrate how one carried a helpless maiden while swinging on a chandelier.

'I see that you, too, are a woman who feels deeply and wholly,' she went on, and laid that slim hand lightly on Mrs Turnbit's mustard-yellow tweed sleeve. 'Someone without pretense; who writes from her heart. Thank you, dearest,' she added, as Emma set down the tray. Though she retained her throbbing 'Camille' voice, the warmth of her smile was genuine. Emma shook her head a little as she retreated to the trestle tables once more. Fifty percent of everything her husband's beautiful sister said and did was about as genuine as the Empress Valerna's jewelry – but the other fifty percent was pure gold.

Even her father would eventually have approved of Kitty.

'Somebody tell Darlene if her butt isn't out here in five minutes—' yelled Madge back through the doors . . .

'So many people' – now Thelma Turnbit was confiding in Kitty – 'only see what I do in terms of . . . oh, of sensationalism, of vulgarity. But it's not, you know.'

'Oh, of *course* not!' Kitty looked shocked at the very idea. Gratified, the columnist smiled and turned her attention to the sugaring of her tea . . .

Emma saw Kitty, in that moment of her guest's distracted attention, throw a calculating glance at the clock by the doors of the stage.

Oh, dear . . .

There was only one circumstance that ever made Kitty conscious of what time it was.

Oh, NOT that good-looking stuntman from Famous Players again!

Timing her response perfectly as Mrs Turnbit looked back at her, Kitty went on, 'Myself, I see what you do as a service. A great sacrifice of time and heart and energy . . .'

'Fer Chrissake who the fuck does Madge think she is?' Darlene Golden strode into the shooting-stage, fragile, fair-haired, and ethereal in her humble (and extremely revealing) slave-girl rags. 'I'm not some friggin' extra, you know. I'm . . .'

She froze beside the trestle tables in the act of removing her stylish lizard-skin pumps when she saw Thelma Turnbit. Then she smiled dazzlingly, stuck her chewing gum on the door frame beside her, and crossed toward Kitty's little encampment, hands held out and radiating all the 'It' she could muster.

She was just opening her mouth to cry an effusive greeting when Kitty got gracefully to her feet and called out through the great doors, 'Madge, darling, Darlene's here!'

'Then get her the fuck out here this frikkin' minute!'

If looks could maim, Kitty's body would have been in pieces on the stage floor.

'*Darling . . .*' Kitty clasped Mrs Turnbit's hand in hers. 'It's been such a privilege – and *such* a pleasure. But now Miss Golden is here at last we cannot make all those good people wait on us. Please do finish your tea. Emma will look after you, won't you, darling? Is there anything else you need? We're all just *terribly* behind schedule . . . *Do* please forgive us . . .'

Without a backward glance, Kitty walked toward the rear doors, where Mary Blanque, the wardrobe mistress, awaited her with a cloak wrought of peacock feathers. Darlene – who like Kitty was in the running for *Screen Stories'* Goddess award – followed perforce, fulminating, behind.

And just as Kitty passed through the door, Emma saw her glance again at the stage clock.

Oh, drat it, it IS that stuntman! Waiting for her someplace . . .

'Can I get you anything else, Mrs Turnbit?'

Or maybe that blond-haired extra from Laemmle Studios . . .

Completely aside from common courtesy, Emma was aware – having been coached by Publicity Chief Conrad Fishbein – that gossip columnists would be almost as eager to have a word with her as with her employer. This would provide an admirable opportunity to pass along a few studio-generated 'confidences' about Kitty's life and loves, Kitty's actual past being best left in discreet shadow.

That, too, she knew, was part of her job. Her husband's glamorous sister had rescued her from the dreary horrors of the Pendergast household at least in part to be a respectable female companion, to keep the fan magazines from saying that Kitty was a tart.

Which of course she is . . .

Like half the other actresses in pictures . . .

She tried to recall whether Mr Pugh was on the lot that day.

Sure enough, the journalist invited her to share another cup of tea, and bent to ruffle Chang Ming's red-gold fur. 'And who are these adorable little creatures?'

While the sweet strains of 'Swan Lake' announced the commencement of scene fifteen (hard upon Madge's bellowed 'Camera . . . *Action!*') Emma made Mrs Turnbit known to Chang Ming and the tiny, five-and-a-half-pound Black Jasmine. ('Yes, he had eye damage as a puppy, poor little chap. It's fairly common, with Pekinese . . . But Miss de la Rose fell in love with him at first sight and he with her, and of course she doesn't care a button that he's half blind . . .') That kindness to the minute dog had been, in fact, Emma's first intimation that there was more to her sister-in-law than gin, cigarettes, and exhausted regiments of discarded lovers.

As usual, shy, flaxen Buttercreme refused to come out of her wicker carry-box ('I have *no* idea what she's doing in Hollywood,' sighed Emma. 'She doesn't approve of the place at all.').

And, 'Oh, yes, those are real diamonds on their collars. Miss de la Rose is so very generous to those she loves.

'She won't admit it, of course,' she added, shaking Mrs Turnbit's hand at the outer door of the vast, barn-like stage, 'but I know she reads your columns faithfully. And, of course, I don't think I have any need to tell you, that though Miss de la Rose is . . . is the most *genuine* person I know' – *no harm laying it on with a trowel* – 'I assure you, she doesn't break hearts and send men to their doom in real life.'

The columnist twinkled. 'I never thought it, Miss—'

'Mrs,' returned Emma with a smile. 'Mrs Blackstone, though please do call me Emma.'

'Oh, yes, the sister-in-law.' The older woman nodded, clearly recognizing the name from the studio releases. She may in fact, Emma reflected, have written a little piece herself, on Camille de la Rose's goodness in taking in her indigent – and highly respectable – English relative. 'But on the subject of breaking hearts, my dear, could you let me know – well, let

my readers know, you understand − if there's any truth to
those rumors about Miss de la Rose and that oil millionaire,
Ambrose Crain?'

She leaned close in a cloying aura of lilac perfume. Not a
pretty woman, and those virulent tweeds and purple hat did
nothing for her complexion, but there was warm and genuine
interest in her small hazel eyes. 'That little piece I saw in
Photo Play a few months ago . . .'

'Completely untrue!' Emma made herself chuckle as she
said it. The last thing Kitty − or anyone − needed was Frank
Pugh going into a fit of jealousy. 'Isn't it amazing how one
can't have a cup of coffee with a friend in Hollywood without
the press trying to marry one off?'

She hoped her rueful twinkle looked more real than it felt.
'I can't imagine where that columnist picked up that rumor.
Mr Crain was a friend of Miss de la Rose's family. Now that
he's spending more time on the West Coast − he owns several
thousand acres between here and Long Beach, you know − he
likes to "treat" her, as he calls it, to an occasional dinner out,
as he used to do when she was a little girl. He's been separated
from his wife for many years, and I think, frankly, that the
poor old man's just lonely.'

Mr Fishbein could certainly have come up with a better tale
than that, Emma reflected. And it wasn't bad for the spur of the
moment. But Ambrose Crain was one of the myriad of subjects
on which it was probably better that the publicity chief − and
Frank Pugh − remain ignorant.

Ambrose Crain, and whoever it was for whose sake Kitty was
suddenly and unaccountably preoccupied with the clock . . .

She shook hands with the visitor ('I can find my own way
to the gate, thank you, Mrs Blackstone . . .') but her mind was
already occupied with the gap of time between scene fifteen
(which involved only two shots that she knew about) and the
extensive sequence (scenes eight through twelve) wherein
the Empress Valerna arrived in Rome − riding an elephant (*did
she ride it all the way from Babylon?*), with dancing-boys in
tow. Setting up for the scenes, and walking through the half-
dozen shots of which each consisted (not to speak of close-ups),
would easily fill the remainder of the afternoon and much of

the night, and it would be best, she thought, if Kitty were under her eye. Just to be on the safe side . . .

Through the great doors she saw that the elephant – whose name was Socrates – had already arrived in the garden. While she had been sorting out the inconsistencies in the original scenario – and dealing with the fact that sometimes individual shots were identified as scenes, which completely dislocated the numbering system – Zal had helpfully provided Emma with a list of which animals were available in Hollywood through which trainers. Properties Chief Ned Bergen had suggested a chariot drawn by zebras, but rumor had it that DeMille was going to use that in a forthcoming film, and Frank Pugh didn't want to be accused of copying the better-known producer.

Ned Bergen's assistant, Ned Devine – Ned the Lesser, he was called – helped her move chairs, make-up, roses, picnic-baskets, gramophone, and pillows to the shade of a couple of beach umbrellas set up just outside the camera-lines. By their third trip scene fifteen was finished – close-ups and all – and Doc Larousse and his minions were shifting reflectors and setting their coffee cups on the bases of the statues again. Emma had left the lap-dogs for last in the moving process, and when she went back to the three little wicker carry-boxes in the echoey cavern of the stage – already being set up for the orgy tomorrow – she found the door of Buttercreme's box open. Both the little dog, and her Russian-leather leash, were gone.

Emma strode quickly to the rear doors and peered through. For a moment she thought she glimpsed Kitty, reassuringly (and a little surprisingly) where she should be . . . then realized that the dark-haired girl in the gauze and diamonds was in fact Kitty's stand-in, Ginny Field. No sign of Kitty herself could be seen in the milling confusion of dancing-boys, wardrobe ladies, men carrying make-up boxes, Babylonian hierophants and a few stray Praetorian Guards. She went back to the other boxes and made sure of her first impression: that Chang Ming and Black Jasmine were still in them, wagging eager tails at the sight of her.

Odd. She'd never known Kitty to walk one of her 'celestial

angel muffins' without the other two. She straightened up, and was preparing to pick up Chang Ming's box when both dogs turned their heads sharply and growled.

At the same moment, Emma's nostrils were assailed by a rancid cocktail of unwashed body-linen, cheap cigars, stale bay rum and even staler whiskey. Turning just as swiftly, she saw behind her in the stage's semi-darkness a tall, broad-shouldered man, the hazy glare of the spring afternoon outside glinting on his slick dark hair.

'Kitty here?' The tobacco-scarred baritone brought a fresh gust of last night's liquor and this morning's coffee. 'Kitty – ah – de la Rose . . .' The glare thrown by a reflector outside showed Emma the fleshy remains of what had to have been dazzling handsomeness at least fifteen years ago. In their pouches of fat, his eyes were cerulean blue, and his tobacco-browned teeth were even and straight. What could still be seen of his original jawline and cheekbones was reminiscent of a Greek god.

Something about the way he carried himself said actor. But any would-be actor in Hollywood – especially on a visit to a studio – would take more care to dress in clean clothes.

Certainly any actor who knew enough about Hollywood to want to make an impression on Kitty.

'I'm sorry.' Emma stepped politely but firmly in front of him as he made to brush past her and onto the garden set. 'She's filming . . .'

'I'll wait, honey. I think she'll see me.' He looked her up and down as if startled to see someone almost as tall as himself in a skirt. 'You tell her Rex is here. And you tell her not to try slippin' out the back way, neither.'

Bootlegger . . .

Emma's heart sank. She knew peddlers of illegal liquor – and worse things – lurked around the studios. A sizeable number of both stars and crew relied on contraband 'pick-me-ups' to get through long days and brutal past-midnight shoots under the hammering glare of the kliegs. Emma had heard from several sources that the Los Angeles Police Department made a comfortable living from graft and wouldn't have dreamed of interfering.

'They'll be shooting, probably, as long as daylight lasts,' she pointed out reasonably. 'So you may be in for a long wait. I'll let Miss de la Rose know, of course, Mr . . .'

'Festraw,' said Rex. 'Rex Festraw. And I don't think she'll make me wait.'

He gave her a grimy sidelong grin. 'She can't have forgotten me. I'm her husband.'

TWO

When she told him, Zal said a word that Emma remembered Jim saying, that time when the motorcar he'd borrowed to drive with her into the Cotswolds one afternoon had gotten a puncture ten miles from Oxford, just as it was coming on to rain. She assumed that it was Yiddish but he'd refused to translate. She made a mental note to ask Zal its meaning, on some occasion when the studio wasn't facing serious scandal.

'Where'd you put him?' Zal asked her now.

'In Kitty's dressing room.' This was in a wing of the Hacienda, the original adobe farmhouse on whose land the studio had been built.

'You lock him in?' Behind him, through those great rear doors, Emma could see Madge Burdon pacing Nero's garden like Napoleon on the eve of Waterloo. The studio musicians, grouped around the plinth of the nearest statue, were playing pinochle and smoking. Emma winced a little at the statue: it was a life-sized plaster replica of Michelangelo's *David*, impressive but 450 years too late for Ancient Rome.

'I did think about it,' Emma acknowledged, and tucked a strand of her mouse-brown hair back into the neat bun at the back of her head. 'But it seemed to me that an irate husband suing the studio for wrongful imprisonment would not help matters. Where *is* Kitty?'

'Looking for Buttercreme.' Zal polished his glasses on another of his clean handkerchiefs. His voice was non-committal. 'She *said*.'

Madge was close enough behind him at that moment to hear this theory, and flung up her hands. 'How long can it take her to catch the damn mutt anyway?' she demanded. 'With those short little legs, the thing can't run *that* fast.'

Miss Burdon had obviously never attempted to corral Buttercreme when the little dog was scuttling for cover. Mary

Blanque of Wardrobe – sitting on Nero's throne sewing fake diamonds onto an extremely abbreviated brassiere – took a peanut from her apron pocket and tossed it to Socrates the elephant. 'She'll be back, honey.'

'Buttercreme?' asked Emma, startled.

'According to Kitty' – Zal's tone remained carefully neutral – 'somebody left the door of Buttercreme's crate open. Kitty dashed off to look for her.'

It IS the stuntman. Or that extra from Laemmle.

'Buttercreme's so timid you could leave the crate open all day and she wouldn't venture out,' protested Emma. 'I can barely get her out to walk her.'

Or maybe that saxophonist she made such a disgrace of herself over last week at the Coconut Grove . . .

'Yeah,' agreed Zal. 'I know.'

'Oh, dear.'

'Could be worse,' he pointed out. 'This *is* Hollywood—'

'I don't believe I want to know.'

He guided her back through the shadows of Nero's half-constructed banqueting hall, and out the front door to the studio 'street'. 'You tell Fishy?'

'He said he'd try to reach Mr Pugh by telephone.' They threaded their way through a forest of light stands and then half a regiment of Louis XV dining chairs outside the main doors of Stage Two. 'But I thought we'd better warn Kitty, so she doesn't return to her dressing room and encounter Mr Festraw unawares.' And – Emma didn't say, but she saw this, too, in her friend's eyes – so that Kitty would have time to prepare a story for the producer's edification.

Zal swore again, but this time his tone was slightly absent-minded, like someone who has encountered a long-petrified hairball behind a couch. 'Fishbein have any idea who Kitty's barneymugging these days?'

Emma sighed. 'He was less than helpful. In fact he suggested we consult the Los Angeles telephone directory, which is *not* fair, *or* true!'

'Oh, Jesus, no. There's a lot of ugly men in that directory.' They stepped close to the wall of the carpentry shop, to avoid a troop of Ruritanian cavalry, on the way to the palace revolution about to erupt on Stage Two. 'You ever heard Kitty mention a kid named Eliot Jordan?'

Emma considered. 'She has a photograph of a very nice-looking young man in her room. I think it's signed, *Eliot.*'

'Damn it. I was afraid of that. Pugh was all set to sign Jordan back in January for eight-fifty a week, which if you ask me is pretty good for a kid of eighteen.' They emerged from between the buildings, crossed the open ground that lay before the Hacienda, and headed for the three-story monolith of the prop warehouse. Emma cast a worried glance at the long, two-story wing of the big former farmhouse that housed the 'star' dressing rooms, but the door of Kitty's remained closed.

'Then Lou Jesperson at Enterprise stole Jordan out from under Pugh's nose with an offer of a thousand. Pugh is still talking about getting after the kid – and Jesperson – for breach of contract, but he'll never make it stick.'

Emma wondered if she should have asked Mr Fishbein to have one of the studio guards keep an eye on the door. Or would that have drawn the attention of Mrs Turnbit, who might very well still be on the lot? She had looked like a woman with extremely sharp eyes. 'How much trouble would there be if Kitty was meeting young Mr Jordan?'

'A shitload.' They turned the corner into the narrow 'street' between the prop warehouse and the commissary, which also housed the make-up rooms. Beyond these stretched the back lot, five acres of standing sets for medieval villages, generic forests, and a noisy construction site where Ned Bergen's myrmidons were, in defiance of the adage, attempting to build Rome in a day – or in any case in a week.

'Frank's in the middle of a divorce – his fourth, I think – and he's like a bear with a hemorrhoid. He's not gonna be thrilled if he hears Kitty's been making nookie between takes with a kid who "betrayed" him. Dang it.' Zal stopped, and looked around him at the extras in peasant garb (and one lost, lone Roman soldier – *Miss Burdon is going to have that one flogged before the Legions . . .*) milling outside the doors of Wardrobe. Men in shirtsleeves came and went between the long sheds of the garage and those of the toybox jungle of the studio nursery.

Emma guessed what he was thinking. The back corners of the prop warehouse, or the farther reaches of the back lot, went unvisited for weeks at a time, and could shelter an army of fugitive lovers.

'Where would you go,' asked Zal, propping his glasses on the bridge of his nose, 'if you wanted to get your ashes hauled?'

'*I* would go to City Hall,' replied Emma, a trifle tartly, 'and get married.'

'Yeah, well, that's exactly what Kitty did,' he retorted with a grin. 'For once in her life. And if she hadn't, we wouldn't be in this mess.'

She couldn't keep from laughing, though she could imagine what her mother – and certainly Aunt Estelle! – would have to say on the subject of Kitty's *amours*. 'Oh, dear, I suppose you're right . . .' *And they would CERTAINLY say that Hollywood – and Kitty – were a Bad Influence on ME . . .* 'All right, then, I'd pick the warehouse. I know there are beds in there, and nobody goes there . . .'

'Are you kidding? Every bootlegger and dope merchant in town uses it for hand-offs.' He opened the building's small side door for her, and flicked the electric switch just inside. 'And anyway, what makes you think Kitty's gonna bother with a bed?' He waved to an unsavory little man sitting on a bejeweled Turkish throne (*MUCH nicer than Nero's!*) in the shadows beside a ferocious-looking stuffed grizzly bear. A small suitcase lay at his feet.

'Hi, Taffy. You see anybody come in here, in the last half-hour?'

'You mean other than that Turnbit broad?' Taffy took his meerschaum pipe from his mouth.

'Mrs Turnbit came in here?' Emma gasped, startled.

'Just put her head around the door,' explained Taffy, in accents that on radio shows (Emma had discovered) seemed to signify inhabitants of the lower depths of the New York waterfront. 'She saw me and took a powder. The door was unlocked,' he explained to Zal, 'on accounta I got an appointment here, see. Meetin' a man about a dog.'

'How long you been here?'

''Bout since two.' He checked a gold pocket watch that was
visibly more expensive than his clothing.

Zal said, 'Thanks,' and led Emma back out. 'Bootlegger,'
he explained as he shut the door behind them. 'Deliveryman.
Works for the Cornero Brothers.'

Emma rolled her eyes.

'Could be worse,' he said again. And then: 'You call a guard
and make sure Thelma Turnbit actually left the lot?'

'No.' Emma felt a flash of embarrassment. 'She said she'd
find her own way out.'

'Yeah, I bet she will. Always call a guard, Em.' Zal patted
her shoulder. 'She's a gossip columnist, it's her business not
to go straight back out of here. She's probably still making
the rounds of her informants on the lot . . . Christ knows how
she got past the gate in the first place. All we need is for her
to spot Kitty and what's-his-name coming out the back door
of Stage Three all rumpled and giggly—'

'Well, they have to emerge fairly soon,' reasoned Emma. 'I
mean, she's got to get back to shoot scene eight before poor
Miss Burdon dies of an apoplexy.'

'Miss Burdon wouldn't die if you shot her with a siege
howitzer.' Zal cast a calculating glance toward the Hacienda
as they emerged into the open again. 'But she *will* get the
Praetorian Guard out after me – that elephant rents by the hour.
Fishy might be able to . . . Dang it,' he added, with another
glance at the Hacienda. 'The Pettingers are here.'

And indeed, Emma could see, on the shaded front veranda
of the Hacienda, a man and a woman, both tall, both rawboned,
both dressed with a frumpiness which was almost aggressive,
in conversation with Foremost's publicity chief.

'Evangelists,' he explained, to Emma's look of inquiry.
'Religious fanatics. They have a radio show, Friday evenings,
and their own church down on Broadway. Champions of
Christian decency and moral censorship. You shoulda heard
'em on the subject of Kitty's last film.'

Recalling some of the more lurid details of *Royal Desire*,
Emma could understand their indignation. In the shadows of
the veranda, Conrad Fishbein – obese, fair, and smiling benevo-
lently behind horn-rimmed spectacles – was holding the door

open for his guests. The female Pettinger – *Brother and sister, or husband and wife?* – drew her skirt aside, as if contact with a 'film person' (as Aunt Estelle would have put it) would give her leprosy.

'What the hell are they doing on the lot today, anyway?' Zal started to say something else, paused, then looked again at Emma as he turned to lead the way toward the garages. 'Are you all right?' he asked.

Am I all right? Emma considered the question, and the letter in her pocket, and the life she'd left behind her in England. *Why is it that everything that happens here is always interrupted by filming or a deadline or a crisis?* Marcus Aurelius, she reflected, would have reminded her that this was no more than to be expected of life . . . Certainly of life *here*.

No wonder everyone in Hollywood drinks.

'It's not anything that needs to be dealt with now,' she said.

'Can we maybe deal with it over dinner at Cole's Pacific Electric Buffet this evening, if you're up to it?' he suggested, a little shyly. 'Depending on how late shooting runs?'

Emma felt the sudden sensation of having stepped back from everyone's histrionic love lives, and onto a little island of sanity. 'I'd like that.' Placing her hand gently on his shoulder, she leaned down a little – a very little – to kiss him. *MORE proof that I'm being corrupted . . .*

She could almost see her mother's frown, and the quick, disapproving shake of Aunt Estelle's head.

'I think probably,' she added, 'you had best get back to Rome before they do call out the Praetorian Guard – or the Ruritanian cavalry. Kitty can't have gone to the backlot. You know how she hates to walk anywhere, even for the sake of love. I have a good view of her dressing-room door from here, and if I miss her here, you can catch her on the set, if you would. We'll just have to trust Mr Fishbein – words I never thought I should hear myself say. If—'

A flash of crimson at the end of the studio street caught her eye. 'There! What did I tell you?'

Like a bird of paradise in her gorgeous kimono, Kitty was headed for her dressing room from the direction of the building where the unused film stock was stored. It took all Emma's

training not to pull up her skirt above her knees and cross the
dusty square at a run, or to bellow Kitty's name, *à la* Madge
Burdon. She walked, however, as if pursued by a troop of
Ruritanian cavalry (or a ferocious-looking stuffed grizzly bear)
and Zal broke away from her and dashed ahead.

Buttercreme, cradled in Kitty's arms, saw them and began
to wriggle eagerly, recognizing friends, and Kitty halted in
her tracks.

'*Darlings!*' She scampered towards them, and Emma ascer-
tained at once that whatever else she'd been doing, her beautiful
sister-in-law hadn't been indulging in a romantic interlude
with an eighteen-year-old actor or anybody else. Her lipstick
and eye-paint were too perfect. 'Oh, thank *God* I've found
you! I didn't *dare* go back to the set with Buttercreme here
and I simply *have* to repair my face! Is Madge absolutely
furious with me? I simply couldn't—'

'Your husband is here,' said Emma.

Kitty froze in the act of shoving Buttercreme into Emma's
arms. 'Clayton?' Staring up at Emma in dismay over the little
dog's head, she gasped the name of her most recent.

'Rex.'

Under a lavish coat of Motion Picture Yellow, Kitty blenched.
'Oh, my God . . . Where is he?'

Emma nodded toward the ersatz Spanish adobe. 'In your
dressing room – I hope.'

'What's he doing here? What does he want?'

'Money, I assume,' said Emma, with a touch of asperity.

'Emma, *please,*' whispered Kitty. 'Don't go all English on
me.' She looked wildly around, as if she expected to see Mrs
Turnbit, notebook in hand, lurking behind the corner of Stage
One. 'This is *terrible!* This is . . . this is *ghastly!* Does Frank
know?'

'I have no idea. Mr Fishbein is trying to contact him, but
apparently some evangelists have arrived—'

'*Here!*' Kitty seemed almost not to have heard her. 'Here
. . . Oh, my God . . .'

Seeing the expression of despairing horror on her sister-in-
law's face, Emma handed Buttercreme to Zal, took Kitty's
arm and steered her back into the shadows around the corner.

'What is it?' she asked quietly. Given Kitty's usually flippant attitude towards former spouses, there was clearly something more here than met the eye. 'How much trouble can he make for you?' Visions of abandoned children, of nameless vices (although most of them, Emma was well aware, had perfectly good Latin names), of drunken vehicular manslaughter flitted before her eyes. 'What would he know about you?'

Kitty stared at her with eyes that seemed even more huge in her delicate face. 'What would he know about me? He'll have our marriage license!' And, seeing Emma's puzzlement at this. 'Emma, I married Rex when I was fifteen. I mean, *really* fifteen, back in . . .' She hastily counted on her fingers, and shuddered at the result. 'Anyway, I've been telling everyone in Hollywood that I'm twenty . . .'

'Ah.' Emma felt a wave of relief. 'So what he could sell to the fan magazines would be the date of your birth.'

'More than that!' gasped Kitty, nearly in tears. 'Worse than that! Because I didn't have my parents' consent I told them at City Hall that I was eighteen, which would make me . . .' She flinched again, and turned her face aside, unable to bear the thought of her real age, not to mention her real age plus three years. 'Oh, Emma—!'

'I'm sure all he wants is money.' Emma wondered how she managed to get herself into conversations like this and what her mother – not to mention Aunt Estelle – would have said. 'It will be embarrassing, but I'm sure, given how popular *Royal Desire* has been, and all the advance interest in *Temptress of Babylon*, Mr Pugh will be happy to come to some sort of arrangement. Mr Fishbein said he'd try to get hold of Mr Pugh, and he can . . .'

She made a move toward the Hacienda, but Kitty caught her arm again in a desperate grasp.

'But what if he tries to make me live with him again?' she demanded frantically. 'What if he demands half – or *all* – of my income for the past nine years? Did he have a lawyer with him?'

'Kitty . . .' Emma frowned, trying to recall what she knew about California divorce law – a subject of perennial discussion amongst Kitty's colleagues. 'Did you ever *get* a divorce from Mr Festraw?'

'I don't know!' Kitty wailed.

Despite her genuine sympathy for her sister-in-law's distress, Emma could not keep from raising her eyebrows. High.

'He said he was going to divorce me when I ran off with Ted,' explained Kitty. 'Or was it Solly?' She counted briefly on her fingers again. 'Anyway,' she continued, giving up the effort, 'I left New York right after that, and then I was in Philadelphia for just a very short time and then Chicago, and for awhile in there I was calling myself Raquelita Vasquez . . . but nobody knows that . . . so if he did serve me with papers, they wouldn't have reached me . . .'

'It sounds' – Zal stepped closer to the two women to lower his voice, Buttercreme trying to hide herself in his armpit – 'like we need to speak to Mr Festraw.'

Kitty's dark eyes shifted. Then she looked back at Emma, and nodded.

But when she didn't speak, Emma asked, more gently, 'Would you like me with you? Or Zal?' The size – the bulk – of Rex Festraw flashed through her mind. Though the first impression anyone received of Kitty – especially on the screen – was one of intense, voluptuous energy, she was, in fact, a small woman, and though curvaceous, rather delicately built. For an instant Emma saw her as she had been at fifteen, married to a man in his thirties who was six feet tall and muscled like a boxer. Her scalp prickled with a rush of angry heat, remembering the smell of liquor on his breath and person.

She's afraid of him.

Kitty bore no scars on her flawless face, but the marks were there in her eyes.

'There's actually no need for you to see him at all,' Emma added. 'I'll get Mr Fishbein, and . . . What's the name of Foremost Productions' lawyer? Mr Spiegelmann? And Zal . . . Might you go tell Miss Burdon that you've found Kitty, but she's been taken ill?' She glanced at her watch. The sky overhead between the stages had the golden tone that suffused California afternoons, and the 'street' was slowly filling with shadow. In a lower voice, she asked, '*Were* you meeting someone?'

'No!' Kitty stamped her foot, her fright of her husband

dissolving into flashing anger. 'I – That is, poor Buttercreme got away – someone must have left her basket open . . .'

Emma opened her mouth to acquit 'poor Buttercreme' of such bravado, but at that moment, Frank Pugh's sleek black Pierce-Arrow pulled in through the ornamental gate on Sunset Boulevard and halted before the Hacienda. The producer climbed out, moving with surprising agility for a man of his considerable bulk, and headed for Kitty's dressing room. He had a small briefcase in hand. Clearly, Conrad Fishbein had reached him by telephone. The publicity chief himself emerged from the Hacienda and hurried to catch him, with a fat man's rolling stride, presumably with a warning about the Pettingers.

Kitty said, 'Oh, nertz,' and darted from the cover of the corner to intercept them both.

'I hope he left somebody in the office to keep an eye on the Holy Twins,' muttered Zal, striding at the star's heels. Emma, making haste to follow, wondered if Thelma Turnbit was still lurking somewhere as well.

Frank Pugh, like Rex Festraw, was a big man. Both were heavily built, dark-haired, and thick with the fleshiness of middle age; the difference being that Festraw had clearly been dazzlingly handsome in his younger days, something which was only said of Frank Pugh by young ladies hopeful of a contract with Foremost Productions. Pugh's eyes, like Festraw's, were light, in his case a cold jade-green and shadowed now by a saturnine scowl as his chief moneymaker scurried up to him, flashing with all the jewels of Babylon.

'Oh, Frank!' Kitty flung herself into his arms. 'Oh, thank God you've come!'

Her acting before the camera was hopeless. But in real-life situations, reflected Emma, her talents rivaled Duse.

'Emma just told me,' sobbed Kitty. 'I was looking for poor Buttercreme – she was clear out in the backlot, poor darling . . .' Kitty's gold-ribboned sandals bore not the slightest trace of the backlot's dust. 'Oh, I thought Rex was dead! I'd heard he'd been killed in a motor accident just after the War. Oh, Frank . . .'

She burst into a convincing rendition of terrified tears, and the producer handed Fishy the briefcase and gently folded her in his arms. 'It's all right, baby,' he said. 'The man probably just wants money and I've got that. There's nothing to worry about.' He kissed the top of her tousled dark head and she raised her face to his, leaving smudges of Motion Picture Yellow on his bosom but having miraculously preserved both her mascaro and lipstick intact.

'Mrs Blackstone.' He fixed Emma with his unnerving green glare. 'Has this Festraw jasper come out of Kitty's room? Or talked to anyone?'

'Not that I know of,' said Emma. 'I've been looking for Kitty – I thought it best that she be located right away, and warned.'

'Good,' he affirmed. 'That Turnbit broad still around? Damn it,' he added, when his publicity chief nodded.

'And the Pettingers—'

'Screw the Pettingers.' He glanced at the dilapidated Pettinger Ford parked in front of the Hacienda beside his own sleek conveyance, as if debating having it hauled away as junk. 'The Pettingers don't bribe my switchboard operators and gate-guards to sell them information.' He put a hand on Kitty's back, and led the way to the arcade that shaded all six 'star' dressing rooms. Kitty leaned into his strength like a schoolgirl clinging for protection, and Emma – joined again now by Zal and Buttercreme – wondered if her sister-in-law's docility was assumed to emphasize to her lover her dependence on his strength, or to make sure that she was on hand to refute whatever her visitor might have to say.

When they reached the second door along the arcade, Pugh put Kitty gently aside. 'If this rube thinks he's gonna put something over on us with some horseshit about still being married to Kitty, he's gonna find—'

He thrust the door open.

Taller than Kitty and slimmer than Fishbein, Emma was just behind Pugh as he took a half-step through the door, and saw the dressing room at the same moment that he did.

And smelled it. The first warm whoof of air that puffed from its stuffy confines.

The smell of gunpowder, that had lingered in her brother Miles's uniforms when she'd unpacked them at his return on leave.

The smell of blood. There wasn't a lot of this. The wounds in Mr Festraw's chest and forehead were small and hadn't bled much. *He must have been killed instantly.* Miles – and Jim – had told her that much about the corpses in the trenches.

The smell of feces was much stronger. Like a lot of victims, Rex Festraw had soiled himself when he died.

Festraw himself had evidently stood up when someone had come into the dressing room, because Kitty's make-up chair was overset beside his body. He looked like he'd staggered back a pace or two and then fallen. The red roses that Ambrose Crain had sent Kitty that morning – only some of which had gone with her to the set – lay scattered about him, like a tribute. He'd been shot in the forehead and the chest, and the gun – a revolver with a long, thick tube attached to the barrel, which Emma deduced had to be a 'silencer' – lay just in front of the threshold.

'Well,' said Kitty, 'damn.'

Emma thought that about summed it up.

THREE

Natura inest mentibus nostris insatialibus, the great Roman jurist Cicero had said, *quaedam cupiditas veri videndi.*

Our minds possess by nature an insatiable desire to know the truth.

Mr Cicero, reflected Emma, had obviously never visited Hollywood.

'Of course it's my gun, Frank, darling.' Kitty raised huge dark eyes to the studio chief as he steered her into Dirk Silver's dressing room next door. 'You gave it to me! But what does that have to do with Rex being dead?'

Silver, ready in cuirass and caligae to welcome the empress in scene eight, looked up startled from the *Volkischer Beobachter* and set down his tumbler of dark amber liquid.

'Was ist los?'

Pugh and Fishbein looked at one another warily, neither quite ready to take the irrevocable step of admitting that anything had happened, and Emma stepped forward and asked, in her schoolgirl German, whether Dirk had heard anything next door.

'Just now?' the star replied in the same language. His dark curls were rumpled and flattened, and the helmet he'd been wearing in scene fifteen hung on the coat rack in the corner. 'Only fifteen, twenty minutes I have been here . . .'

He glanced at the clock – Pugh made damn sure there was a large clock in every dressing room – and then at the gun in Fishbein's hand, without much interest. Prop guns could turn up anywhere on the lot. But his brow darkened at the sight of Zal and Kitty. 'Where they been? They've had the set ready to go for an hour now and Madge is shitting broken bottles—'

'You heard nothing?'

'Heard what?' The German's frown deepened. 'What's up?'

'Get him outta here,' ordered Fishbein, when Emma relayed this information, but Pugh caught Silver's arm in a hard grip as he turned to get his cloak and leave.

'He stays here. Fishy, stash that gun in the trunk of my car, and make sure you wrap it up good in something. And have a look through the room for anything else that looks shady. I'll be with you in a minute. You.' He jabbed a finger at Silver. 'Stay here.' He pointed to the floor, turned back to Kitty. 'You didn't know Festraw was in town?'

She shook her head, hugging Buttercreme to her chest as a child will hug a toy for comfort. The Pekinese, not liking the producer's tone, gathered all her courage and challenged him with a sound much like that produced by a small rubber duck when it's trodden on.

'I didn't even know he was still alive!' Kitty's eyes filled with realistic tears.

'What's going on?' asked Silver again, in German.

Zal responded – in much better German than Emma's, 'Feller was shot in Kitty's dressing room.'

'You!' Pugh swung around on the cameraman. 'You don't tell him a thing! Not a thing! Tell him something was stolen from Kitty's room, a bracelet or something.'

'*Erschossen*?' Silver exclaimed.

Zal held up a warning hand in the star's direction, but Silver poured out a torrent of questions and speculation, which fortunately the studio chief did not understand. But when Silver strode towards the door, Pugh stepped in front of him, poked with his finger again. 'You tell this kraut to stay put, Rokatansky. All of you stay put.' He glared at Emma and Kitty. Buttercreme barked at him again from the safety of Kitty's kimono.

Faithful to the legal principles of the Roman Republic, Emma began, 'Surely the police—'

'I'll deal with the police. When was the last time you heard from this four-flusher, Kit?'

'Not for years!' she protested, and Emma saw her hastily counting back in her mind and on her fingers. 'Not for – oh . . .'

'When'd you dump him?'

Kitty was spared further mental arithmetic by the opening of the door. 'I found these, boss.' Fishbein, the gun still in hand, held out a couple of crumpled pieces of paper. 'They were in his pocket. I thought you'd better see them.' Emma caught a glimpse of the elaborate gold curlicues which decorated her sister-in-law's private, personal notepaper that nearly filled one drawer of her bureau in the dressing room. *From the Desk of Camille de la Rose, Foremost Productions, Hollywood, California*, not that Kitty had ever sat down at a desk in her life. The engraving of the Hacienda at the top, and the gold scrollwork that surrounded it, occupied a good thirty percent of each page's surface. Emma could just imagine Aunt Estelle's reaction, should she receive a reply to her letter inscribed on such a sheet.

You shall never have a penny of my money, was written on one in a girlish scrawl. *I hate you and will have nothing to do with you. Leave me alone or I will shoot you dead.*

Come near me and I will kill you, said the other.

One was dated April 14th – which had been Monday – the other, yesterday, the 15th. Both were signed, *Camille*.

'Oh, come on!' Zal snatched the papers from Pugh's hand as the studio chief took them to read. 'You can't really think Kitty did it. She can't hit the side of a barn at three feet.'

'I can, too!' Kitty protested.

'You really shouldn't touch those,' pointed out Emma, as Kitty stepped past her and seized the notes from Zal. 'I'm sure the police are going to want to—'

Pugh took them back, ripped them into pieces, and handed the pieces to Fishbein. Fishbein took the ashtray from Silver's dressing table (Silver rescued his half-smoked Chesterfield in passing), tossed the litter of stubs and ash out the door, then dropped the evidence into the china dish and lit it. 'Find anything else?'

'Not so far.'

'I didn't write those!' Kitty's fingers shook as she took the tumbler of whisky from Dirk Silver's hand and drained it.

'Nobody's gonna say you did, sugar.' The studio chief laid a soothing hand on her shoulder. 'But you gotta come clean with me. Where were you between . . . What time did she leave the set, Rokatansky?'

'We finished scene seventeen at quarter after one,' reported

Zal. 'Then Miss de la Rose talked for about twenty minutes with Thelma Turnbit—'

'What the hell was that broad doing on the lot in the first place?' Pugh turned sharply to his publicity chief. 'Who let her in the gate?'

'No idea.'

'Well, get an idea. All we need is for *her* to get hold of this . . .'

Furious thumping on the door. Madge Burdon's voice boomed through the panels, 'You in there, Kitty? For Chrissake, if we don't get something in the can we're gonna have to bring that frikkin' elephant back tomorrow at twenty-five bucks a—'

'Beat it!' yelled Frank back. 'Miss de la Rose is indisposed!'

'That you, Frank?' demanded the director, unimpressed. 'What are you, doin' a threesome in there? I didn't know Dirk was your type.'

Fishbein stepped outside, and shut the door again.

'I swear it!' Again Kitty lifted those limpid, tear-filled eyes to her lover's. 'I'd left my cigarettes in the stage, and while Madge was having the lights moved, I went back in and saw that someone had left the door of poor Buttercreme's basket open.' She hugged the little dog closer. 'I hunted for her *everywhere*! I finally found her out in the back lot, near the peasant village sets—'

Outside, Emma heard Madge exclaim, 'Fuck no! If I'd sent anyone out looking God knows when they'd be back—'

'When'd you last see the gun?' Pugh turned back to Kitty.

'I don't *know*!' Her voice shook and she dabbed at what Emma guessed were now genuine tears. 'Not for over a year!'

Given the clutter of kimonos, divan, chairs, liquor cabinet, cushions, make-up shelves, old fan mail and fashion magazines that crammed her dressing room, this was not difficult for Emma to believe. *You could probably conceal Socrates the Elephant behind the shoe-rack . . .* Behind her, Dirk Silver and Zal were still engaged in explanations in German too swift for her to easily follow, but she did catch the words, *Kitty? Sie konnte keinen Heuhaufen schlagen . . .*

'Did you put that silencer on it?' asked Emma. 'And did you ever take it out of the dressing room?'

'Good heavens, no! I mean, I don't know. I don't *think* so . . .' Kitty looked inquiringly at Pugh, as the door opened and Fishbein slipped in again, still holding the gun under his jacket.

The studio chief explained, 'About a year ago some nut broke into Mae Busch's place in the middle of the night. The couple who did Kitty's gardening had just quit, and she hadn't gotten anybody else to live in the cottage—'

'But I never *did* take it to the house,' put in Kitty. 'I mean, I was supposed to get a license for it, or a permit, or something, and we were right in the middle of filming *Sawdust Rose*, and I just never got around to it. There wasn't a silencer on it when you gave it to me, was there, Frank?'

'What do we do about the body, Frank?' asked Fishbein quietly. 'The gun's one thing. Do we cop to it, or not?'

'Hell, no!' He turned back to Kitty. 'Nobody was with you looking for pipsqueak there?' He nodded to the little dog still cradled in her arms. 'You didn't get the Duchess to help you?'

'I sent her to see Mrs Turnbit to the door,' reported Kitty promptly. 'And I thought I could find my little treasure right away. I couldn't *imagine* she'd get that far!'

The studio chief's eyes narrowed, but Emma could see him studying – as she had – the pristine state of the star's make-up and drawing the same conclusion that she had. Whatever Kitty had been up to in the almost two hours that she'd been gone, she hadn't been kissing anyone. Which, come to think of it, reflected Emma resignedly, was a little unusual in itself . . .

'And you didn't write those notes?'

'I swear it, Frank! I didn't know Rex was in town! I didn't know he was *alive*!'

'Anyone could have gotten the stationery from her dressing room,' pointed out Emma reasonably. 'And the gun, for that matter. The room isn't kept locked during the day.' She restrained herself from making the observation that were the evidence not at that moment dwindling into a little pile of ashes, they might have had the handwriting compared against Kitty's, for forgery.

The brief glimpse she'd had of it hadn't looked much like the star's.

'You,' said Pugh. 'Rokatansky. What the hell's he yakking about?' He jerked his head at Silver.

'Just asking what's going on,' replied Zal.

Silver declared protestingly, '*Wenn ein Mann durch eine kapitalistische Verschwörung ermordet wurde . . .*' and Emma sighed. She had wondered how long it would take the handsome German to conclude that there was a capitalist plot involved in the murder.

'You tell him nothing's going on. You tell him there was a little accident with one of the maintenance boys who went in to fix the sink in Miss de la Rose's dressing room, but that the man's fine and has been sent home. You got that?'

Zal nodded at once. 'Sure thing.'

'*Kapitalistische Schweine . . .*'

'You. Duchess.' Pugh rounded on her. 'You too, Kitty. Mrs Blackstone went with you lookin' for your little mutt – Zal, you went along, too. You found the pooch and brought it back. You didn't see anything, you didn't hear anything.' He glared at them with his bulging, pale-green eyes. 'If anybody asks questions about it – cops or reporters or anything – you were out in the back lot from one fifteen to' – he checked his watch – 'three thirty. I'll get a couple of the prop boys to say they saw you out by the Rome set. Got that? Fishy, how much of a mess is there on the floor? How long'll it take to get the bloodstains out?'

'That's gonna be a problem, Frank.' Fishbein shook his head. 'There's not a lot of blood, but it soaked straight through the rug and I'm betting it's stained the floorboards underneath—'

'We can get a new rug.'

'Vinegar or baking soda should take care of the stain,' provided Zal helpfully.

'Problem's gonna be getting the body out of there,' said the publicity chief. 'We'll need to keep the place locked until the lot's cleared tonight, and *Scandalous Lady*'s shooting overtime on Stage Two, to make up the time they lost when—'

'Send 'em home,' said Pugh. 'Tell 'em the wiring on Stage Two needs to be checked overnight 'cause there's danger of fire. Better yet, get in there and set a fire, just enough to burn about a square yard of wall. And dig up somebody who can be trusted, to help with moving the stiff. And I mean somebody who can be trusted not to come around later with his hand out. You empty his pockets?'

'Surely the police—' began Emma again, but the producer rounded on her again with those cold protuberant eyes.

'No police,' he said. 'Didn't happen. Or anyway it didn't happen here. You remember that, Duchess, or you're gonna be on the first boat back to England—'

'As it happens—' retorted Emma, nettled, and Kitty sprang to her feet and stood between her lover and her sister-in-law like a diminutive ornamental pigeon pecking at a bulldog.

'Don't you *dare* threaten Emma, Frank! She doesn't work for you, she works for me! And I won't have you bully her!' She slipped a protecting arm around Emma's waist. 'I mean it. If you try to send her away, you can finish your silly picture by yourself! And that goes for you, too, Fishy.'

Pugh opened his mouth, then closed it. Conciliatingly, Conrad Fishbein set the gun down on the make-up table and took Emma's hand in his own plump sweaty ones.

'Mrs Blackstone,' he purred in his most persuasive tone, 'I apologize for the misunderstanding. It was entirely my fault that you should misconstrue what we're asking of you. This is purely a precautionary measure, and a purely temporary one, to avoid adverse publicity. Surely you've been in this country long enough to know how the newspapers, and particularly the film magazines, will distort facts and take any statement out of context, with destructive and, I may say, irresponsible results.'

Behind thick lenses, his wide blue eyes gazed earnestly into hers. 'Mr Pugh and I are very familiar with this kind of sensationalism, and as a personal favor, I'm asking you to trust our judgment. We will, of course, get in contact with the police and turn the whole thing over to them at the proper time. But in an environment like Hollywood, in the light of sometimes unscrupulous competition from other studios who would like nothing better than to see *Temptress of Babylon* halt production indefinitely, we need to have a clearer picture of what's going to be said, and how the situation is going to be handled, before we simply let everyone in on today's events. Don't you agree?'

He looked from Emma's face to Kitty's.

'And of course,' he added, 'the studio will compensate you for the inconvenience and upset that I know this must be causing you.'

Emma glanced at the final curl of smoke rising from the ashes of the two notes, while behind her, Mr Pugh instructed Zal in an undervoice to inform Dirk Silver that his Bolshevik arse would be on the first boat back to Germany if he said one word about any of this to anyone. Or, possibly, that he might find himself in trouble with the Bureau of Investigation . . .

'I'll let you know,' Fishbein went on in a helpful voice, 'when it's time for you to make a statement, and the whole thing may be easily settled by a written affidavit, without you having to be further troubled at all. Nor, of course, Miss de la Rose.'

Pugh's eyes were on Emma's face. He must, Emma guessed, be a past master of reading those small details of expression and tension that told him when he'd won an argument, or whether he needed to change tactics. Now, after the pause that followed Fishbein's words, he said in a mollified tone, 'Thank you, Mrs Blackstone. Fishy, you better get over to Stage Two and give 'em word to clear out. Get Gully Ackroyd to come over here and help with the Dear Departed. After this last time getting fired, he knows he'll never work again unless he does us a big favor . . .'

Emma wondered if this meant that she would not, in fact, be obliged to rewrite scenes twenty to twenty-four, but did not think it the moment to ask.

Fishbein was already heading toward the door.

'And tell Floyd at the gate to make sure the lot is cleared by six.'

The publicity chief scooped the gun from the make-up table, opened the dressing-room door, and found himself face-to-face with the apostolic Pettingers.

Prudence Pettinger stared at the gun in Fishbein's hand and gasped. Her brother fell back a pace, shocked.

Veritas nunquam perit, that other great Roman, Seneca, had said.

Truth never perishes.

Frank Pugh, under his breath, said a word that could easily have taken the hide off a charging rhinoceros.

FOUR

The police arrived twenty-five minutes later.
'They can't *possibly* arrest me!' Kitty paused, half-in and half-out of the stylish walking dress that Emma had fetched from Wardrobe. Knowing that the star's dressing room would be sealed, she had borrowed a garment which had made its last appearance in the train station scene of *Faithful Nell*, rather than permit her sister-in-law to go down to the Sixth Division station house in a diamond-studded brassiere and a pair of spangled briefs that wouldn't have concealed a packet of cigarettes.

Now, looking out the slatted jalousies of Nick Thaxter's dressing room on what Americans called the second floor, Emma would not have bet any substantial sum on Kitty's being right. In rewriting a scenario at the end of last month (*Lost Lamb*) she had learned enough about the examination of bullets to be fairly certain that the slug someone would eventually dig out of poor Mr Festraw could be traced to Kitty Flint's gun.

And once the Pettingers had seen that gun in Conrad Fishbein's hand, the jig – as Zal had observed – was definitely up. Trying to conceal the crime at that point would only make everything look a thousand times worse.

So Mr Pugh had been dispatched to call the Los Angeles Police Department, while Mr Fishbein (after ostentatiously placing the gun on the *Volkische Beobachter* spread out across Dirk Silver's make-up table) had taken the two evangelists to his office to ascertain what they may have seen and heard – other than the fact that the publicity chief had had the murder weapon in his hand. And Emma had sought alternative costume.

'Oh, and I look *ghastly*!' continued Kitty, regarding herself in Nick's mirror. 'Can you come do me up the back, darling? Film make-up is so *hideous* . . . Oh, my poor little darling!'

She ducked from Emma's helpful hands to kneel beside
Buttercreme, who was attempting to conceal herself under the
make-up table. 'Don't be afraid, sweetness! Nothing bad is
going to happen . . . Zal, darling!' She darted, still exposed
from sacrum to fifth cervical vertebra, to the door as Zal
appeared in the long window.

'Would you be a complete *darling* and get Addie from
Make-Up to come here? And bring my kit from Stage One.
Oh, no, it's out in the garden now, isn't it? Nick has *absolutely*
nothing here in my shade . . . Oh, except this lipstick . . .'

Through the open door – from the dusty square below in
front of the dressing rooms – Pugh's voice boomed up, 'Ask
her what the hell's taking her so long!'

Considering how long the producer had known Kitty, Emma
was a little surprised that he'd ask.

Three police cars were now parked in front of the Hacienda
and it was all Ned Bergen and Mack Farley – the studio's
Head of Security – could do, to keep the extras from gathering
around to gawk. Since Thaxter's dressing room was directly
above Kitty's, Emma could hear the muted grumble of voices
below as plump Lieutenant Meyer and cadaverous Sergeant
Cusak examined the scene.

'I think they can,' affirmed Emma, catching up with her
sister-in-law and doing up buttons. 'And I think they're going
to, unless you can prove where you were. I know you can't
have been in the back lot because neither your dress nor
Buttercreme's fur has even one foxtail caught in it.'

She picked up the Empress Valerna's discarded robe and
held up the sequined hem. Even in the well-trodden purlieu
of the main studio compound, trailing gowns, cloaks, and silk
stockings were forever picking up the barbed, arrowhead-
shaped seedpods that grew so abundantly in California. Emma
daily extracted half a dozen from each Pekinese's fur while
brushing them.

'They don't grow *everywhere*, darling,' said Kitty uncon-
vincingly, and sat down at the mirror, to mop cold cream on
her face. 'I *swear* I was just looking for—'

'Whatever you were doing' – Zal slipped through the door
and shut it behind him – 'I think you're going to need a better

story than that. Lieutenant Meyer just found three letters from Rex Festraw, dated the beginning of last week, shoved in the back of the top drawer of the vanity in your dressing room, Kit. I thought Pugh was gonna give birth when Meyer brought 'em out.'

Kitty's mouth popped open in a shocked O. 'But I never *got* any! I really, honestly, never got any—'

'If you'd just tell us—' Emma began, and her sister-in-law shook her head vigorously, and went back to clearing the pale-yellow maquillage from her face.

'It had nothing to do with Rex. In fact it had nothing to do with anyone. I was looking for—'

'Oh, come on, Kit!' insisted Zal.

Emma's brow puckered. 'Why would anyone want to frame Kitty?'

Zal raised his eyebrows and glanced towards the French door. Beyond the walkway outside – and past the railing – Emma could see Darlene Golden scamper across the open ground between the stages and the Hacienda, clothed not in her scanty slave-girl rags, but in even-more-revealing veils from another film entirely . . .

And she, clearly, had removed her camera make-up and put on the rouge and powder she would have worn on an evening out with a beau.

Frank Pugh came out a few steps to meet her, and Darlene threw herself into his massive arms.

Emma met Zal's eyes.

An ambulance van and two more police cars turned slowly through the studio gates from Sunset Boulevard. The guards who let them in sprang to intercept the dozen men – some with cameras – who had been crowded up against the gates arguing with Floyd. Zal sighed. 'Terrific.'

'Frank won't let them arrest me.' Kitty swiveled around from the mirror. Without the thick coating of Motion Picture Yellow and powder, she looked older, and a little fragile. Hollywood, Emma was coming to understand, could be very hard on those who lived there, and she often found herself worrying about this beautiful, maddening goddess who loved her dogs and had made sure that Emma had been invited to

the studio Christmas party within a few weeks of her arrival,
and who never got enough sleep. 'We're three-quarters of the
way through filming, and he would *never* start reshoots this
late! It would cost a fortune!'

Down below, Darlene clasped Frank Pugh's hand, pressed
it to her bosom, and (Emma was certain) assured the studio
chief that she, Darlene, would stand by him with unshaken
loyalty and love through his coming time of trial.

A uniformed officer was briefly glimpsed coming out of the
main office, then disappeared again under the arcade, clearly
headed in the direction of Kitty's dressing room below. Zal
asked, 'Want me to see what Winged Mercury found out?'

'No,' said Kitty. 'I want you to get Addie and my make-up,
and take poor little Buttercreme, put her in her box, and take
all three of them back to my house. Poor darling, this is so
upsetting for her.' She bent down, picked up the little dog,
and carried her to the French door where Zal and Emma were
still looking out, though thankfully Pugh and Darlene had
disappeared back into the arcade. 'She's so sensitive, I'm afraid
all this is going to make her ill! And poor Chang, and my
darling little Jazz, must be wondering what on earth became
of me.'

'They're not the only ones.' Zal took Buttercreme into his
arms.

Emma put an arm around Kitty's shoulders. 'If you're in
any trouble—'

'I'm *not*! I was just looking for—'

Detective Meyer and two policemen appeared at the end of
the second-floor walkway, trailed by Conrad Fishbein and Al
Spiegelmann, the lawyer for Foremost Productions. Down
below, Frank Pugh's voice could be heard snarling, 'Get these
people out of here!' and a moment later he, too, lumbered up
the steps from below, dark face surly. To Meyer he said, as if
continuing a conversation, 'That coulda been anybody phoning
anybody . . . Rokatansky, you tell that kraut muscle-boy if he
says one word to those newshounds, I'll see to it his contract
is terminated and his commie ass is on the first boat back to
Germany.'

Down below, the reporters were scattering from the

menacing bulk of Mack Farley and three studio guards. Some trailed after Madge Burdon, striding off in the direction of Stage One. Others clustered around the ambulance, doubtless waiting for the coroner's men to remove Festraw's body. The Pettingers, pushed to one side, approached one or another of the reporters – undoubtedly with the intention of stating their own convictions about the moral turpitude of Hollywood. But, Emma observed, they were being ignored, a state she knew would last only for as long as it took for the police to remove Kitty from the scene.

At that point, she guessed, they would become the center of attention.

Detective Meyer was a short, stout, balding man whose lumpy face was adorned with the style of beard favored by film villains: a black-dyed van dyke with absolutely symmetrical flashes of white at the corners of his mouth.

'Do you identify the dead man as your husband, Rex Festraw?' He flipped open his notebook as Pugh shut the dressing-room door on the noise from below. Crammed with Fishbein, policemen, and Spiegelmann (who'd been shut out and had to be admitted once Pugh realized it), the room put Emma forcibly in mind of either a sequence from one of the less demanding two-reel comedies which Foremost produced over on Stage Three, or of the sort of exercise undergraduates at Oxford found hilarious.

'You don't have to answer.' Fishbein wormed through the press to Kitty's side.

'Former husband.' Kitty drew herself up like the Empress Valerna staring down St Peter in scene fifty-eight. 'I have not seen him since before the end of the War.'

'You received no communication from him?'

'None.'

Meyer produced and unfolded three sheets of letter paper. Looking over Kitty's shoulder, Emma glimpsed the words: *I'll come around on Wednesday and if you don't have $10,000 it'll be the worse for you.* Another proclaimed: *I can spill secrets that'll have you on the street by next week.* 'That his writing?'

'Good Heavens, how would I know?' Kitty turned back to

the mirror and appropriated a jar of Nick's moisturizer. 'I only ever saw it on IOUs, and that was . . .' She stopped herself from any specific revelation about how long it had been since her days as Mrs Festraw. 'That was just *years* ago.'

'Where were you this afternoon between one fifteen and three thirty, Miss de la Rose?'

'I was looking for my *dog*.' She returned her attention to the contents of Nick's make-up drawers. To Emma, these appeared to contain almost as much high-quality rouge, mascaro, and powder as did Kitty's own.

'You didn't get a telephone call in your dressing room at two ten?'

The question startled her into looking up. 'I wasn't *in* my dressing room at two ten.'

'The studio operator says a call came through for you at that time. A man's voice answered – in your dressing room, so presumably that was Mr Festraw – and said, Yeah, she's here, and called you to the phone.'

'The operator actually heard Miss de la Rose's voice?' asked Emma.

Meyer glanced at her, not troubled at being interrupted, and shook his head. 'She says she doesn't listen to calls.' He glanced sidelong at Pugh. 'Says she'd get canned if she did.'

'She's gonna get god-damned canned anyway—' growled the studio chief.

'Anybody go on this dog hunt with you, Miss de la Rose?'

Kitty's chin came up defiantly, and Spiegelmann put in, 'You don't have to answer any of these questions, Miss de la Rose.'

'Nobody was with me.' She flicked a glance at Pugh, who flushed an alarming shade of turkey red. Returning to the mirror, she began applying rouge. Fortunately, reflected Emma, Nick Thaxter's skin tones were reasonably close to Kitty's. 'I don't usually have to take along a bodyguard to find my poor Buttercreme when she gets lost, any more than I need somebody sitting at my bedside all night, in case somebody should accuse me of murder at three in the morning. People *do* do things by theirselves, you know.'

And a story that involved Emma and Zal accompanying her,

Emma thought with relief, could be too easily checked . . . particularly by the Pettingers.

Kitty dusted powder on her face, and pursed her incomparable lips to dab on the reddest shade in Thaxter's extensive collection. 'And you can't arrest me,' she added, 'because I really didn't do it. Is there *any* mascaro in there that matches mine, darling?'

Detective Meyer refused to let anyone besides Al Spiegelmann ride down to the Sixth Division Police Station with Kitty. Emma secured a ride in Frank Pugh's big Pierce-Arrow, clinging to the leather hand-strap in stoic alarm as the furious studio chief roared out onto Sunset Boulevard like a Roman chariot out of the starting gate. The reporters – ejected by Mack Farley and his myrmidons – scattered before him, having clustered around the gates like ants around a jam pot. As they swept full-tilt into the traffic on Sunset, Emma caught a glimpse in the crowd of what looked like Thelma Turnbit's purple hat and mustard-colored tweeds.

Since she'd stepped from the train last October into the Moorish fantasia of Los Angeles' Santa Fe station, Emma had periodically experienced the sensation that she'd wandered somehow into a dream – except her own dreams were generally far more prosaic, involving the purchase of broccoli at the market or the cataloging of Etruscan inscriptions. But looking at the anger-darkened face of the man beside her, the cold set of the heavy lips – remembering the sharp, business-like bark of his conversation with pale, plump, oleaginous Mr Fishbein and the curl of smoke from Dirk Silver's ashtray as they burned evidence – the sense of being in a dream of some kind returned. A frightening dream, as it sank in on her: *he doesn't care. A man died, shot to death, and he simply doesn't care.* It was literally no more to him than poor Mr Ackroyd getting drunk and being fired from the picture: an inconvenience. *Here, Duchess, you rewrite scenes twenty through twenty-four and it never will have happened.*

Reporters beat them to the station house. Emma supposed they'd telephoned ahead. 'The bail bondsman should be here already,' Pugh snapped, thrusting his way before her to the doors – the first words he'd addressed to her since, *Get in the car.* There was no sign of either Mr Spiegelmann or Kitty in the station's reception area, but a tall, golden-haired, extremely handsome, young man in a double-breasted suit sprang to his feet as they entered, and moved straight to the studio chief.

'Colt Madison.' He thrust out his hand. 'Mr Fishbein told me to meet you here.'

Emma took a seat on one of the wooden benches, already occupied by a fat, angry looking man in a cheap tweed jacket that smelled of very stale meat. Three reporters pressed briefly against the glass of the outer door, but had evidently been told to stay out in no uncertain terms. Beyond them, the last of the California daylight threw shadows almost all the way across Cahuenga Boulevard, and flashed on the windscreens of passing cars. Somewhere in the station, a woman insisted, 'I *never* told him he could stay! He said he just needed a place to sleep for two or three nights . . .' Elsewhere, a typewriter clattered, a telephone rang.

That home would be yours, Aunt Estelle had written, of the green, sweet, familiar quiet of Oxford.

Emma closed her eyes.

It wouldn't be the same, of course. She knew those long evenings would never come back, when she'd helped her father with cataloging all those small and intricate fragments of inscriptions painstakingly copied in Italian ruins, the endless minutiae on variant medieval versions of Livy and Polybius. In the spring of 1914 he'd been planning to return to the purported Etruscan ruins in the Apennines, which would have been Emma's first field experience. As late as 1916 he'd still spoken as if it would take place. *When all this is over . . .*

At Aunt Estelle's, she knew, she would be expected to be a sort of senior daughter in the household, a role she was well prepared to play: acting as housekeeper, helping to arrange dinners, chaperoning her cousins when they came 'out'. She would be the person she had all her life planned to be.

Like Odysseus, she thought, when he finally made it home from Ithaca and cleared out all Penelope's importunate suitors . . . *Although presumably I won't have to kill anybody . . .*

Tidying up loose ends. Finding those he had loved in his former life . . . Except that her father, unlike the wanderer's, would not be there to welcome her back.

But his work will be, she thought. Scholarship, friendship, the world she had known . . .

And at least nobody will hand me a farrago of a half-written scenario about Babylonian empresses (!) coming to 'corrupt' first-century Rome!

Someone came onto the lot and killed a man in Kitty's dressing room . . .

She opened her eyes again, and saw Frank Pugh, towering over Detective Meyer, beating his hand on the corner of the sergeant's desk to emphasize his words.

She wondered where Kitty was.

On her twenty-sixth birthday – this past September – Emma recalled that she'd been making plans to kill herself. She'd known exactly how to go about it. The Romans were very helpful about such matters. *Eripere vitam nemo non homini potest,* Seneca had written. *At nemo mortem; mille ad hanc aditus patent.*

A thousand doors open on to it . . .

She had planned to wait until Mrs Pendergast went out to her married daughter's for afternoon tea. Then she'd steal a razor from Lawrence Pendergast's room, fill the first-floor bathtub with hot water (the one in the attic never got remotely warm), lie down in it, and slit her wrists. (Longways, the Romans advised, so there was no chance of a small cut closing up again.) Early authorities were almost unanimous in saying that the method did not hurt much.

Not nearly as much, she had concluded, as Mrs Pendergast's constant, resentful fault-finding; as Lawrence Pendergast's assumption that any woman who worked for her living was lawful prey.

Not as much as the pain of living without her parents, without her brother . . . without Jim. As the knowledge that there was nowhere for her to go.

But that was the day that Kitty had come flouncing up to the Pendergast door, trailing an aura of gin, cigarettes, and dissipation, fresh off shooting *Passion's Smoke* for Minerva Films in

London and in quest of someone to come back to America with her to brush her Pekinese and balance her checkbook and give her a much-needed halo of respectability.

That evening, to her own astonishment, Emma had found herself getting on a boat. It had felt very odd.

The next day she had laughed, for the first time in what felt like years.

Laughter had almost hurt.

I can't leave her. Not at this moment.

She drew a deep breath, and felt as if Aunt Estelle's letter – fluttering in the back of her mind like an outraged pale moth – retreated to a shelf marked, *To Be Dealt With Later.*

'That's horseshit!' roared Pugh. 'Kitty – Miss de la Rose – didn't even know the sap was in town!'

'Then what was he doin' with two letters from her in his room?' returned Meyer calmly.

Opening her eyes, Emma saw the detective shift his dark gaze from Pugh to the handsome Mr Colt Madison with a kind of smug wariness.

'That was Officer Cusak on the phone. I sent him over there the minute we got his address out of Festraw's wallet.'

Judging by the producer's expression, Emma guessed he would have words to say to Mr Fishbein about not burning the contents of the wallet along with the other evidence.

'They found two letters from Miss de la Rose on the table at Festraw's place. Pretty strongly worded, I gather. Cusak's on his way over here with 'em now. One of 'em said, and I quote' – he produced a notebook from his pocket and glanced at it – '"Come near me and I will kill you".'

Pugh's fist slammed the corner of the desk. 'Those were a goddam plant!'

'Are you implying that the police' – Meyer's voice was deadly quiet – 'would manufacture evidence, Mr Pugh?'

Madison stepped forward, leading with one shoulder as if squaring up for a fight. 'Wouldn't be the first time in this town, Bub.'

Oh, good. Emma got to her feet. *Let's get the police angry at us . . . If the wily Odysseus could deal with an irate Cyclops and hungry Laestrygonians,* she reasoned, *I can certainly deal with one studio chief and a mere detective of the Los Angeles Police . . .*

She stepped forward as Meyer was opening his mouth, and said, 'Please excuse me, Detective Meyer, but might it be possible for me to see Miss de la Rose for a few minutes?' Short of snapping, *Get lost, sister*, neither Meyer nor Frank Pugh could very well continue the brewing battle. Both turned to look at her – Emma thought Mr Madison looked a trifle miffed at being upstaged – and she went on in the firm tones she had used when encountering drunken undergraduates on the High Street. 'Whatever decision is reached about Miss de la Rose's status, I know she'll have instructions for me concerning her household affairs. I would very much appreciate it, if you could spare a few minutes for me to see her – under whatever supervision you consider appropriate, of course.'

Meyer went to the office door in a corner, presumably to ask a sergeant for permission. Madison – whoever he was – turned to Pugh and said, without any effort to lower his voice, 'Don't let these goons put one over on you, Mr Pugh. Those letters are a plant. Raymer' – he jerked his head at the sergeant's door – 'would like nothing better than to pin a big one on a movie star – or get the leverage to hit you for a fortune, to make the whole thing go away. Don't let him make a monkey out of you.'

'*Nobody*,' grated Pugh, in a voice just as carrying, 'makes a monkey out of me.'

Emma had known Frank Pugh as a powerful man, an intimidating man: a man whom Kitty used as casually as, by her own account, she'd used one or two of her husbands and any number of her admirers. A protector and a source of silk dresses, diamond bracelets, and caviar suppers. There had been something almost comical in the way the glamorous screen star deceived him. But now, looking at him, Emma shivered. He was not, she realized, comical at all, and Kitty was playing with fire.

Behind her, Zal Rokatansky's voice asked quietly, 'What's up?' He stood at her elbow, make-up case under his arm.

She felt exactly as if she had stumbled and, in the act of falling, been caught by strong arms.

Before she could speak his glance went past her and he
said, 'Jesus Christ, Colt Madison!'

'Who *is* he?' She could not help noticing that Madison,
while speaking to Pugh, kept one eye on the glass in the
doorway of the sergeant's office, which reflected the room . . .
and himself.

'Just about the least competent private investigator in LA,'
said Zal. 'But the most photogenic. How's Kitty? Are they
booking her? Ambrose Crain' – he named the smitten millionaire whose crimson roses had glorified Kitty's dressing room
and her base camp in Stage One – 'turned up just after Pugh
left, and gave me a lift up to the house to drop off the celestial creamcakes. He's waiting in the drugstore across the
street, in case Kitty needs a ride home. He was all ready to
shell out for bail on the spot, but I told him Pugh would
probably take care of that. And I brought the paint box.' He
patted the make-up case. 'Nick's rouge a little too pink for
Kitty?'

In spite of herself, Emma stifled a giggle. 'Now, don't speak
ill of Mr Thaxter *or* his rouge! He was *very* generous to let
us all invade his dressing room.'

'Wouldn't dream of it. And don't get me wrong, the rouge
looks great on him. And how are *you*?'

'Holding up,' said Emma. 'A little to my own surprise.'

'Not to mine.' He gave her a shy grin. 'I'll back a proper
educated Englishwoman against the Keystone Kops any day
of the week.'

'Don't be so sure of that.' She glanced worriedly in the direction of the watch-room's street door, as the lugubrious Sergeant
Cusak entered and crossed straight to the door of Sergeant
Raymer's office. Beyond the windows, the sky was losing its
light. Street lamps, yellow in the California dusk, blossomed
along the sidewalks; the drugstore window on the other side of
the street flung a garish carpet of light over the sidewalk and the
faces of the passers-by. 'Evidently Detective Meyer sent a man
immediately to Mr Festraw's lodgings and they found letters
from Kitty there—'

Zal made the same remark he had made earlier in the day,
when apprised of Rex Festraw's presence on the lot. 'More

of 'em?' he added after a moment. 'That's quite a correspondence . . .'

'And the letters said, "Come near me and I will kill you".'

'Fuck me. I mean, Gosh. That's got to be a plant.'

'Even Mr Madison seems to have figured that out,' agreed Emma. 'The identical words . . . But it makes me wonder who would go to such trouble to have Kitty accused of the crime . . . and why are they doing such a bad job of it?'

FIVE

I t was well after midnight when Frank Pugh dropped Kitty and Emma off at Kitty's miniature pseudo-Moorish villa, far up Ivarene Street in the Hollywood Hills. Only the stars, and the distant glow of an enormous, lightbulb-plastered sign advertising a failed real-estate development called HOLLYWOODLAND, illuminated the velvety blackness. Sagebrush and dust gave the dry air an exquisite savor that Emma would forever associate with California; the eyes of small animals, foxes or coyote, glinted out of the dark. 'I *do* hope poor Ambrose understands why I needed to have Mr Pugh bring me home,' Kitty said, as they mounted the high steps of the porch, and waved after the departing headlights of the studio chief's car. '*Please* wake me tomorrow in time to telephone him . . . Christ, I need a drink! Zal?'

In the Stygian shadow where the ground sloped sharply down from the street, round spectacle lenses caught the porch lamp, very much like the eyes of the smaller prowlers above.

The cameraman emerged from the darkness, where his battered pre-war Ford had been tucked behind the big eucalyptus tree at the turn of the drive. While Kitty had been cold-creaming Nick Thaxter's not-quite-flattering cosmetics from her face – in the back office generally used, Emma suspected, for the questioning of recalcitrant suspects – and Al Spiegelmann and the bail bondsman were negotiating with the precinct jailer, Detective Meyer, and a district court judge, Zal had asked Emma softly, 'Does this whole business smell as fishy to you as it does to me?'

'You mean that telephone call to the dressing room?' She'd set down the nearly illegible carbons of the booking forms and the police report, suddenly aware that she would cheerfully have done murder herself for a cup of tea. 'Or the duplicate letters in Mr Festraw's rooms? Somebody knew she'd be away from her dressing room at two ten – and knew that Mr Festraw would be there. Hiding that set of threatening letters in the back of her bureau, most likely.'

'And somebody'd been in earlier,' pointed out Zal, 'to swipe the gun and the stationery. God knows how he managed to find the gun. And whoever he was, he came back when he knew Festraw was there, which means he was watching the place – if it *was* a "he" – and had co-ordinated times with whoever made that phone call. It was a set-up, all right, and a pretty careful one.'

'Yes,' agreed Emma quietly. 'So why was something so carefully arranged done so badly?'

'Darling,' Kitty had called out, 'could you give me a hand? This stupid lamp is worse than a klieg light and I can't see a *thing* in the mirror . . .'

In the corridor outside the little interrogation room, Colt Madison's voice had rattled like a well-modulated typewriter, pouring out his own theory – conspiracy by figures high in the government and police department of Los Angeles – with a rehearsed lucidity that never so much as stopped for breath, let alone to search for a word. It was like hearing an actor declaim – 'the whole object of creating scandals like these is to draw attention to the need for censorship of the medium' – a river flowing freely, rather than an ordinary human's speech.

'Good thing it was,' pointed out Zal, turning over the booking sheets. 'Or else our girl would be spending the night in the slammer, and then Pugh and Madge really *would* have coronaries. They don't usually give bail on a murder charge.'

The last form in the pile, Emma had seen, had set a special hearing for the twenty-eighth.

'I *told* you they wouldn't arrest me,' Kitty had declared, and before Emma could explain to her that they *had*, in fact, arrested her – and that she had only a combination of studio clout and police corruption to thank that she wasn't going to spend the night in the cells – Pugh, Fishbein, Spiegelmann and Detective Meyer had returned, filling the little room and all talking at once. Zal had slipped quietly away, presumably to cross Cahuenga Boulevard to the drugstore and let Kitty's lovestruck millionaire know that his services wouldn't be required.

But Emma had not been at all surprised, to glimpse Zal's car in the shadows of the eucalyptus tree as Frank's big Pierce-Arrow had turned down the steep drive. And now, as he emerged from the darkness and approached the high, tiled steps of the house, she saw that he carried an assortment of small paper bags and boxes, and wafted about him the astonishing scents of egg foo yung and chop suey. Kitty squealed in delight and flung her arms around his neck, at the risk of getting lo mein sauce on the studio wardrobe's dress, 'Darling, if you weren't in love with Emma I'd marry you on the spot!' She kissed him on both cheeks. 'I can't *tell* you what it means! I'm absolutely *dying*—'

She scampered ahead of them up the steps, and Emma, pausing to relieve the cameraman of some of his awkward burden, whispered, '*Thank* you!'

'Would you like a drink?' called Kitty over her shoulder as she entered the house – surrounded immediately by her three miniature guardians – and made a beeline for the elaborately carved Chinese liquor cabinet. 'Oh, Zally, did you make sure to tell Mrs Shang to feed . . . Oh, I see you did!' She put her head briefly through the door into the kitchen. 'The gin is nothing to worry about – my bootlegger tells me it comes *straight* in from Canada, not like that *awful* bathtub rotgut they serve at the Dome café . . .'

'Hey,' protested Zal good-naturedly, following her across the tiled floor of the dining room and down the five steps to the kitchen. 'I know the guy who runs in the Dome's supplies and those come from Canada, too.'

'Well, he should be reported and locked up for fraud, then.' Kitty rummaged in the cabinet. 'Or attempted murder . . .'

She followed them down, a bottle of Tanqueray and three glasses in hand. 'Not that any of them ever tell the truth. Did you tell poor Ambrose what was going on, Zal? I saw his car as we drove off the lot, with those *awful* detectives . . .'

'I did.' Zal spread the paper boxes out on the table as Emma filled the tea kettle. 'I told him Pugh has already hired a gumshoe but that I don't think much of him. He says he'll put up whatever cash we need, to get to the truth. He said – and I agree with him' – he held Kitty's chair for her, then started opening boxes – 'that if whoever really killed Festraw works for Foremost – or for one of the bigger studios, Universal or UA – we might not be able to trust our Fearless Leader to give a straight story to Meyer and his boys.'

Emma, her hands full of plates, hadn't thought of this. It was like discovering that Patroclus had really been spying for the Trojans. 'Oh, dear!'

'But why would somebody who works for Universal or UA want to kill Rex? Do you want any of this, darling?' Kitty paused, gin bottle in hand. 'No . . . Zal? More for me, then . . .'

'If they actually wanted to get Kitty out of the way,' pointed out Emma, 'they'd have made those notes more convincing.'

Zal took a bottle of olives from his pocket, opened it and handed it to her. 'If we knew any of that,' he said quietly, 'we'd have a better idea of what we need to watch out for . . . if anything.'

'Watch out for?' Her glance went from Zal to Emma and back again. 'Watch out for what?'

'We don't know,' said Emma gently. 'We not only don't know who killed Mr Festraw, but *why* he was killed. But the facts that have come to light so far: the telephone call to your dressing room, at exactly the moment when you weren't there; forged correspondence from you to Mr Festraw and vice versa; the fact that whoever killed him did so in your dressing room when there are probably ten thousand less conspicuous places in the Los Angeles area where it could have been done; all tells us that it was worth somebody's while to arrange his murder in exactly this fashion. Mr Spiegelmann would tear the case against you apart in court.'

Kitty sat down in one of the kitchen chairs, and fished, rather blankly, in the pockets of her dress – which, having come from Foremost Productions' wardrobe department, didn't contain a single cigarette. Emma opened the kitchen drawer that contained the household supply. Both the Shangs smoked like chimneys. Zal lit a kitchen match and held the flame to the cigarette as Kitty took it, but his glance crossed Emma's. 'And whoever's behind this,' he pointed out quietly, 'would know that.'

Emma said, 'Yes.'

She was silent, as Kitty thought this through.

'I think,' Emma went on after a moment, 'that until we get some idea of who *is* behind it – someone, I assume, with a good deal of money – I would suggest that none of us, whatever we find out, talks to anyone about it, until we've talked to each other. Not Mr Crain, not Mr Pugh, not Mr Spiegelmann . . . nobody.'

Zal said, 'I agree,' and Kitty, after a swallow of gin, nodded.

'The way people blab in that studio, God knows where *anything* will end up. You know, just the other day when they were getting ready for the banquet scene with Nick – *darling*, did the Romans really eat things like swans and mice? No wonder they died out! – I heard one of the wranglers – the *wranglers*, dearest! – tell an extra about me and that *gorgeous* young man in the wardrobe department up on the catwalk above Stage Three . . . and *nobody* knew about that . . .'

'Presumably the gorgeous young man did,' pointed out Emma.

'Yes, darling, but he'd never let it on to anyone because Connor Stark – that's his agent, you know – is *terribly* jealous, and would disown any of his young men who so much as *looked* at a girl . . . though I don't see why *he* should care. Not to mention all those *stupid* stories about Mr Crain taking me to dinner that ran in *Photo Play* . . . But it just goes to show you—'

She picked a fragment of lobster from one of the plates, handling her chopsticks as if she were the Empress of China rather than Babylon. (The motion picture industry, Emma had observed, seemed to survive on Chinese take-out. Zal was teaching her to wield chopsticks, one of several skills – along with mixing cocktails and tallying baseball scores – which she had not expected to learn in America.)

Emma refrained from pointing out that in fact Mr Crain *had* taken Kitty to dinner, repeatedly . . . And one never knew when columnists were watching.

'But that brings us back to the question,' she said. 'Why would someone who worked for Foremost, or Universal, or anywhere for that matter, want to murder Mr Festraw? He looked very down-and-out, and of little use to anyone, though

ces might be deceiving. And why would
ied for the deed?'
rk eyes widened. 'I didn't have anything

...body's going to a lot of trouble,' observed
Zal, 'to make a lot of people think that you did.'

'That's *silly*,' said Kitty firmly. 'And anyway, like he said
in the car, Frank isn't about to let $250,000 worth of filming
get washed out to sea.'

From the moment they'd gotten into Pugh's Pierce-Arrow
outside the Sixth Division station – leaving Al Spiegelmann to
hunt for a taxi for himself – the studio chief had poured forth
his plans to deflect bad publicity, and to paint Camille de la
Rose as the wronged, martyred woman struggling to clear her
name ('*And believe me, baby, some of that evidence sounds
pretty hinky to me.*'). 'Don't cry, baby,' he'd said, taking one
hand from the wheel to put it around Kitty's shoulders as she'd
wept – convincingly – with gratitude on his chest. 'It's one
thing for the papers to go after a big lug like Arbuckle for rape,
or make a stink about some director's shady past when he's
knocked off. Fishy'll make Festraw the villain, persecuting *you*
. . . we'll get the papers to drag in how the police are persecuting you as well.'

Now, poking thoughtfully around in the egg foo yung with
the end of a chopstick, Kitty said, 'Ambrose is a major stockholder in the Hearst chain and Scripps-Howard.' For all her
appearance of a scatterbrained flapper, Kitty had an unerring
instinct about where money came from, and where it went. 'I
can't imagine someone like Lou Jesperson over at Enterprise
would think he could push Frank into selling the studio to
Enterprise, just by causing a scandal over me. Even if he *does*
have that slick tramp Anita Tempest under contract. He has
to know Fishy would use a mysterious accusation like this
one to make me even more *fascinating* with the public, than
to hurt me. Especially since the handwriting on those silly
letters doesn't look a thing like mine.'

'You get a look at them?' asked Zal.

'The ones that Mr Pugh *didn't* burn?' Emma couldn't keep
herself from adding.

'Oh, yes. That awful flat-foot practically waved then. my nose. I said, if he doubted my word, he can check against my contract and a whole bunch of things I've writ. at the studio.' She frowned, and her dark eyes grew distant as she considered the implications of the evidence.

'Darlene would want me out of the way,' she said at last. 'She's ready to do murder, to get herself elected the Goddess of the Silver Screen in that *Screen Stories* contest . . . and to get her claws into Frank. I guess you could say the same for the others – Anita Tempest and Gloria Swanson and Clara Bow and Peggy Donovan, though I will say I wouldn't think Peggy would do something like that. Screw Lou Jesperson, yes. But I don't think she'd do dirty to a friend. Well, not that dirty. And that new girl Norma What's-Her-Name at Goldwyn. And I hear Theda Bara's trying for a comeback . . .'

'But would any of them,' pursued Emma, 'actually *kill a man*, to get *you* out of the way?'

'Gloria Swanson,' replied Kitty promptly, 'would kill a man who beat her to a taxi-cab.'

'Don't be silly, Kitty,' put in Zal. 'Swanson never takes taxis.'

'Well, that's true. But whoever wins that *Screen Stories* contest is going to make headlines in every photo-play rag in the country. If I could get an extra two thousand a week on my contract, or an extra film . . . or make a comeback if I hadn't made a picture in a couple of years . . . I'd sure kill Rex for it. Even if he *hadn't* been my husband.'

Emma considered for a moment. The impossible probable, Aristotle had said, is always to be preferred to the improbable possible. Mostly, her father had generally added, because we seldom actually know the limits of the impossible.

So what are we actually looking at here?

Aristotle – and her father, studying a chart of the Etruscan ruins at Orvieto – would have said, *Start with what you know.*

'Tell me about Rex,' she said. 'How long did you know him?'

Kitty counted on her fingers. 'About six months.'

'And how long after you married him?'

'No,' she said. 'In all. I mean, we were really hardly married at all . . .'

'Did you love him?'

'Oh, *passionately!*' Kitty clutched her bosom and raised her face to an imaginary key-light. 'I was crazy for him – he was *gorgeous*, and *amazing* in bed. This one time, just after I got the job with Ziegfeld, he came home with three bottles of cognac and a Hungarian lion tamer . . .'

'And *that*' – Zal held up a finger – 'is all we need to know about *that*.'

'Oh, I suppose so. But I honestly didn't know that people could *do* things like that.' Her face clouded. 'It's hard to tell, you know, looking at someone who's dead, when the last time you saw them they were alive . . . But he didn't look like a Greek god anymore, did he? You said you talked to him . . .'

'Briefly,' said Emma. 'And, no. The years hadn't been kind to him.'

'Good.' Old anger briefly quenched the old pain in the dark eyes. And behind it, a flicker of remembered fear. 'He always drank, you know. More than he let on, when he'd come to the stage door. He could hold his liquor better than anyone I've ever seen, at least he could then. I think he was really trying to catch Lillian Lorraine – the dancer, you know – between husbands. But he and I . . .' The fatigue-bruised flesh around her eyes puckered again, as if she'd accidentally leaned her elbow into an open safety pin, and she took another long drag on her Camel.

Emma recalled what Jim had told her, about what his parents had said of his younger sister's leave-taking.

'Well, I'd just left home.' She exhaled a thin line of smoke. 'And I was living with three other girls in a fifth-floor walk-up on Pearl Street, and I was wild to get out of there. One of them had given up the stage completely by that time and I'd come home and find three of her boyfriends all sitting in the front room – which was where I was supposed to sleep – all sort of glaring at each other, while she was in the other room with number four. She kept trying to get me to do a sister-act with her, and I *wouldn't* go back to my parents, even if they'd take me. And Rex had a really nice apartment, and lots of money – at least, then he did. And, like I said, he was *phenomenal* . . .'

She waved the recollection away, as if in those days, at the age of fifteen, she hadn't been terrified at where she knew it would end.

'You know, sometimes we were really rich. I'd have a maid, and he'd have a valet, and we'd have a cook, which was a good thing, because I wasn't any better in the kitchen then than I am now . . . And we'd live in these beautiful apartments in classy buildings like the Ansonia and the Apthorp, and go out to dinner every night. But then the jewelry he'd buy for me would sort of disappear, and he'd announce we'd have to move, to these *awful* dives in Harlem or Brooklyn. He was a gambler, and he'd get into debt with the gangsters over on Eleventh Avenue – that's when he wasn't buddies with them, lining up rich patsies for their card games. I guess you'd call him a stage-door johnny.'

It wasn't what Emma would have called him, but she held her peace.

Kitty sighed, and drew in another lungful of smoke. 'He knew everybody on Broadway, and all the respectable out-of-town businessmen who'd come to New York looking for a good time. He was an actor himself – he was in *The Spring Maid* – so they were flattered as hell. He'd either cheat them himself, or steer them into scams or crooked games or Gyp the Blood's whorehouses, and he'd get a percentage of the take. I was working the whole time – either for Ziegfeld or in the line with *A Winsome Widow* – but some of the men he'd have over to drink when I came home scared me. I don't mind tough customers . . .' Her eyebrows, still dark with mascaro, dipped again, making that angel face suddenly old, and weary. 'But these guys . . . You'd look in their eyes and there was nothing there. Just . . . like beads. And a lot like beads, some of them, with their pupils all down to a pinprick from dope. I remember one of them got angry at one of the others – I don't remember why, but it was something silly, like who was opening pitcher for the Giants that Sunday or something like that. He knocked him off his chair and kicked him, then picked up the chair and beat him with it, beat him 'til he broke his ribs and his pelvis, while all the rest of them just sat and watched. Rex included.'

She ground out what was left of the cigarette on the saucer that Emma silently handed her. 'The rest of them, it was just a day's work to them. And for all I know the bastard really deserved it. He could have robbed orphans or beat his wife or burned down hospitals for the insurance money. But Rex didn't do a thing, because he was scared.'

She fell silent then, as if she had returned to that tiled apartment kitchen, pressed up against the wall beside her handsome husband's chair, watching one man beat another almost to death on the floor. For a time the only sound was the tick of the clock, which read quarter past one.

Emma found herself remembering Frank Pugh's heavy features, red with anger but set and almost expressionless. *'You didn't see anything, you didn't hear anything . . . Didn't happen . . .'*

Zal asked, after a time, 'Why'd you leave him?'

'He was jealous.' She looked up at them, returning to the present. Her real self, Emma thought, without the overlays of the gorgeous maneaters she played, or the dazzling, flamboyant star who figured in every screen magazine in the country as the glittering embodiment of 'It' (*Whatever 'It' is . . .*). With just a trace of a defiant sixteen-year-old girl who realizes that she's in over her head and has no place else to go.

'Like he had any business bellyaching about *my* love life . . . When he was sober he'd yell at me about even *talking* to other men . . .'

Her beautiful eyelids lowered for a moment as she concentrated on lighting another cigarette, made Emma certain that talking was not what her sister-in-law had been doing . . .

'But when he got drunk, he scared me. One night we got into an awful shouting match, when I came in late. He said he was sick of being married to a tramp, he was going to throw me out on my ear. Well, I'd already heard he'd been out on the town with Minnie Mazzola – she was a vaudeville singer and the sweetest person . . . she had a lot of money, too, so I knew he was sort of looking for a reason to divorce me so he could marry her. So I said not to put himself to the trouble, and I put on my coat again – the most beautiful chinchilla, silver-gray and black: Ruggy Breevoort bought it for me . . . Or was it Bottles Findlay? – and I walked out of the flat. It was four in the morning and it took me forever to get a cab on Ninth Avenue, but I went to a friend's flat, and a few days later I left town with Solly Rosengo, who danced at the Tivoli and had just gotten a job at the Silver Shoes in Jersey City . . . Or was it Ted?'

She counted on her fingers again. 'But I never saw Rex again,' she finished, with the air of one virtuously returning to the subject at hand. 'He'd been pretty sober when we had our fight, so I knew he meant it, when he said he'd divorce me. And frankly, considering the kind of people he ran around with, I'm a little surprised he made it all the way up to this afternoon.'

'Do you know anything about his family?' asked Emma after a moment. 'Or where he was from originally?'

'Oh, New York, I'm pretty sure. And to hear him tell it, his family had been well-off, though he sometimes said he'd been to Yale, and sometimes to Princeton. He was always telling me I was just like his mother, which I don't think was supposed to be a compliment. I always thought he was sort of like me – the family had some kind of money, but gave him the bum's rush for some damn thing. And frankly, I was just as happy to get out of New York at that point, because to be honest I was always a little afraid I'd run into my parents, or Jim, or one of Papa's rabbi friends on the street – not that I ever *was* on the street during the daytime.'

And all during that time, reflected Emma – during Kitty's brief, tempestuous marriage and her career as a showgirl on the Great White Way – her older brother Jim, after a discreet name-change from Blechstein to Blackstone, had been studying, first at City College and then at New York University. Like his sister, he had sought to shake free from his scholarly father's expectation that the only proper use of education was to become a rabbi.

He'd been a year from his degree in architecture, when he'd been drafted.

That tall, young man in American uniform, black curly hair falling into his eyes as he gazed around a fashionable shop in the Regent's Arcade. Then he'd shyly approached her, asked,

'Excuse me, miss, but . . . could you spare a minute to help me pick out something for my sister?'

The sister who at that moment had been surreptitiously packing her bags in preparation to leave her third husband (or, as it turned out, the man she *thought* was her third husband) to head out for Hollywood . . .

The sister he had written to in secret, without their parents' knowledge, for years.

The sister he had never ceased to love.

Kitty stubbed out her cigarette, poured herself another gin, kissed her and Zal goodnight, and went up to bed. 'Of course Frank isn't going to stop the shooting and I've got to be in costume by seven . . . I suppose it would make more sense to stay up than to get up, but it isn't fair to you, Zally, or to poor Emma. Frank's going to send a studio car for us . . .'

She blithered for another fifteen minutes about how they all really should get some sleep, before Emma finally herded her up to bed. Coming downstairs, she found Zal still in the kitchen, Chang Ming snoring like a fluffy red-gold bear in his lap. Zal gently shifted the little dog to another chair without waking it, rose, and picked up his cap. 'Anything else you need?'

'Other than three more hours of sleep than I'm going to get?' Emma smiled ruefully. 'I trust Mr Pugh is going to hand this Mr Madison *carte blanche* to question everybody in the studio about whether they saw either Kitty, or anybody else coming or going from her dressing room? Or heard a shot between two ten and four this afternoon?'

'Good luck with that.' Zal poked his glasses more firmly onto the bridge of his nose as he followed her across the living room, with its chromium furniture and Chinese antiques, and out the front door. 'You could probably shoot off a gun *without* a silencer and people would figure it was palace revolutionaries warming up for scene sixty-seven. We have close to four thousand people working on that lot, plus probably 300 extras, between *Temptress of Babylon* and *Scandalous Lady* and the comedies over on Stage Three.'

'And that's not even counting people like your friend Taffy in the prop barn.'

'I forgot about Taffy.' Zal grinned. 'Not that Taffy would

hurt a fly.' It was very late now; a night bird in the abyssal shadows of the hills whooped a strange, eerie cry. Emma saw the reflected glow of the lamp in Kitty's bedroom vanish from the leaves of the eucalyptus tree. She felt suddenly, absolutely exhausted, and the thought of getting up again in four hours was like sandpaper on her nerves.

'But Kitty's Number One Boy sounds like he could have pretty much anybody after him,' Zal went on after a moment. 'Except I think you're right. Why drag Kitty into it at all? Why not take Mr Festraw up to the mountains and shoot him? Or drop him off the Venice Pier at four o'clock some morning? Unless there's somebody so obviously pissed at Festraw the cops would land on him – or her – first thing, if he was just found in some bean field in the Valley.'

'Then why not do a better job forging her handwriting? The samples I saw didn't look a thing like hers. Why set up something as obvious as a love tryst to keep her busy – because I'll swear that's what it's going to turn out to be . . .'

Zal slowly shook his head. 'But you're right about one thing,' he said. 'We don't know who's passing along information to who, or why. There's a lot of money in this town, Em, and everybody from the mayor to the shoeshine boy is on the take from the studios and the bootleggers. The head of the Vice Squad used to run the biggest prostitution ring in town.'

Emma shivered. Her months in Hollywood had given her a front-row seat on an astounding display of the misuse of power, and there were far worse things to spend money on than fountains of bootleg champagne at one's parties or solid gold door-handles for one's car.

'Whether Kitty murdered her husband or whatever else she was doing for those two hours, what's going to matter at the hearing is what somebody *else* wants to happen . . . for reasons we have no idea what they are.'

He took her fingers gently in his, and lifted himself – a very little – on the balls of his feet to kiss her lips. In a film, Emma reflected with a tiny inner smile, Madge would have had him stand on a box.

'See you in Babylon,' he said.

She stood on the high porch and watched him descend the steps, cross the drive in the yellow California moonlight, and – after a suitable cranking and grinding and advancing and adjusting the old Model-T's spark – drive slowly up to the road, and vanish into the blackness of the hills.

SIX

L OVE'S FATAL TRAGEDY! sobbed the headline in the
Examiner.
'I like that,' approved Zal, when Emma brought it –
and a cup of coffee – to the empress's garden at eight thirty
the following morning. 'Fishy's a better writer than most of the
people cranking out scenarios in this town.'

'The same could be said of Black Jasmine.' She unfurled
the *Times*, which trumpeted, THE SILVER SCREEN
MURDER across the front page, accompanied by a studio
publicity shot – *not* a snap from the sidewalk outside the Sixth
Division police station – of Camille de la Rose. Personally,
Emma was a little surprised they'd managed to find one that
made Kitty look tragic and hunted (though still heart-stop-
pingly beautiful) instead of like a *femme fatale.*

Fatale, she reflected, was *not* the image that people needed
to see at the moment.

'Looks like Crain got right on it.' Zal sipped the coffee
gratefully, keeping a watchful eye on the assembled Nubians,
Praetorians, and dancing girls, similarly reviving themselves
on the palace steps. Knowing exactly what he sought, Emma
also made a mental note of coffee cups and cigarette butts.
Madge Burdon – chain-smoking like the Dark Satanic Mills
of Manchester – had the look of a woman who didn't need
the news that scene ten would require yet another retake
(elephant and all) because someone had left a half-burned
Chesterfield on the pedestal of Michelangelo's *David.*

'You should've seen the headlines about the pink nightie
somebody found in Bill Taylor's bungalow when he was
murdered,' he went on. 'I heard Paramount dropped Mary
Minter as soon as they could do it without a lawsuit – it was
supposed to be hers. The scandal went on for months.'

'According to this' – Emma refolded the paper to the inner-
column continuation of the story of poor 'Camille's' shock,

prostration, and tremulous courage in going on with shooting of *Temptress of Babylon* – 'Mr Festraw was mixed up with bootleggers, both in New York – where he's evidently been living – and here. Somebody on the *Times* must have stayed up late wiring the East Coast.'

'Or else they made it up.' Zal set down his cup and took the paper. Madge glared at her watch, glared at the gates, and glared at Zal, though until Kitty was finished with her make-up and came across to the set there wasn't much the cameraman or anyone else could do. They had already set up the lights and reflectors – Ginny Field, a bathrobe over her copy of the empress's diaphanous black-and-gold gown, now made up the fourth of the musicians' endless pinochle game by the David statue. 'It sounds a lot like what the publicity boys at Goldwyn came up with, about drug dealers murdering Bill Taylor because he was about to turn stool-pigeon. Though from what Kitty said last night, it could actually be true about the late lamented.'

Madge swung toward the big stage door like a gun dog scenting blood, but it was only four soldiers of the Praetorian Guard, grumbling curses about Colt Madison's wholesale enquiries in the studio canteen.

The detective had already set up shop there when Emma and Kitty had arrived at the studio gates at six thirty, and was systematically grilling everyone who'd been on the lot the previous day about where they had been and what they had seen between one forty-five and four p.m. By seven, Madge had been ready to do murder herself. So had Ned Bergen, who had barely a week to complete the Burning of Rome set and whose workers were being held for special questioning about small dogs and crimson kimonos.

When Emma had gone to the canteen for coffee, the line of gaffers, riggers, women from Wardrobe, and extras had snaked around amongst the tables and almost out the door, reminding her of a somewhat eccentric East End soup kitchen. Six old-fashioned Victorian dressing-screens – borrowed from the prop warehouse – formed a sort of cubicle in one corner, and from behind them, Madison's clear, sharp voice could be heard: 'So what time did you come out of Wardrobe? And what route did you take to Stage Two?'

'Which is silly,' Emma had remarked to Kitty, when she'd returned to the dressing room with her tray. Actually to Nick Thaxter's dressing room, now a jumble of make-up kits, kimonos, costumes, shoes, and astrology magazines . . . Poor Nick had been moved in with Marsh Sloane for the time being, to the great alarm of them both. 'There are whole categories of people who couldn't possibly have seen anything: the entire camera and lights crews of *Temptress*, to begin with, and everyone working on *Scandalous Lady*. Plus Mr Sloane and Miss MacKenzie and Miss Violet . . .' She had named the principal players of the Ruritanian epic. Down below, a little gang of prop men swarmed in and out of Kitty's room, bearing buckets and holystone and the remains of the bloodstained carpet.

'It's silly because I wasn't *anywhere*!' Kitty had insisted, pouring gin from her flask into the coffee. 'I mean, I was in the backlot looking for my poor little creamcake . . .' She'd cast a melting glance at Buttercreme, visible as nothing more than a leash and a few strands of ivory-pale tail, trailing out of the wicker crate.

In a corner, Chang Ming and Black Jasmine had stared at one another in hostility over a marabou slipper, like two wigs readying to do battle.

Emma had opened her mouth to point out that she was perfectly well aware that so far as she knew, the carpenters at work on Rome had seen nothing of the studio's major star – in a crimson kimono and four square inches of sequins, she'd have been difficult to miss – and then closed it. She read the defensive glint in Kitty's eye, and the tightening of those fragile shoulders, and knew that contradiction would only result in a display of mulishness that would make Scenes Nine through Twelve even later than they already were.

Entering the garden now, trailed by Mary Blanque bearing the peacock-feather cloak (in itself easily worth more than the salary of all the extras put together), Kitty looked fresh and bright-eyed – astonishingly so, given how little sleep she'd had. As she hastened to Madge, grasped her hands and begged her forgiveness with her beautiful smile, Emma retreated with the newspapers to the little camp outside the string-marked boundaries of the shot, and settled into Kitty's chair. On location, she had at times doubled her chores as scenarist by acting as script-girl, but on the lot, it was usually Herbie Carboy, Zal's assistant, or one of the extras, who would hold the clapperboard. So she was free – if 'free' was a word applicable to anyone on a film set – to peruse the articles regarding the quietus of Rex Festraw.

Zal was right, she reflected. The enamored Mr Crain had clearly used his influence at both the *Examiner* and the *Times* (and to a lesser degree the *Express* and the Hearst-owned *Herald*) to slant the accounts of yesterday's events to emphasize mysterious tragedy and the victimization of a plucky and dazzling film star, rather than the somewhat bald fact that Camille de la Rose's ex-husband had been found shot dead in her dressing room, with her gun. *Stunned as much by the sudden shadow arising from her tragic past, as by the terrible shock of the discovery itself, Miss de la Rose nevertheless insisted on accompanying detectives to the Hollywood Division station to assist with their investigations . . .*

No hint whatever that the weapon had been hers.

The *Herald* contained a full-column letter from Bushrod Pettinger denouncing the moral turpitude of the West Coast Babylon (right next to a half page extolling the latest models of ladies' underwear), but Emma sensed that not only Mr Fishbein, but the all-powerful Mr Hays of the Motion Picture Producers and Distributors Association, had been at work to soften the scandal.

In the past few years, Emma gathered, there had been scandals enough. Where there was room to turn this one from a sordid melodrama to a Gothic tragedy, it would be done.

At least, she reflected uneasily, so long as Kitty had Frank Pugh's support.

She returned her attention to the *Examiner* article, and the skimpy paragraph at the bottom that gave details about Rex Festraw's (1880–1924) life. He had, indeed, been born in New York, and was described as an actor, though no stage credits were given to support this assertion. They had been married 'during the War' (which Emma knew wasn't true) and Festraw was described as deserting 'Camille', also not true – no date given. *In the end, after searching in vain for word of the man who, in spite of his treatment of her, she still loved, Miss de la Rose had no choice but to file for divorce on the grounds of desertion. In her heart, she told this reporter, she believed him dead, and for many dark months was consumed with grief.*

In that, Emma also detected the fine hand of Conrad Fishbein.

She glimpsed Mr Fishbein's influence as well in the insinuations that Mr Festraw – 'an habitual drunkard and wife-beater' – was mixed up with gangsters and bootleggers in New York and had undoubtedly come west to get into the smuggling business. For weeks, it said, he had been harassing his terrified ex-spouse with threats which she gallantly threw back in his face.

'All right, you guys,' yelled Madge. 'Remember you're pagans! You *hate* these goddam Christians! They tried to murder the empress who's frikkin' *paying* you! She gets killed, and you'll all be suckin' sidewalk!'

Emma looked up, her attention drawn to the gaggle of extras assembling behind the great bronze doors which had already done years of service in British castles, Egyptian palaces, and French dungeons . . . rather, she reflected, like the extras themselves. Clothed in rough tunics, tattered dresses, and the occasional more patrician toga, they had stormed fortresses, fled in panic from invading Huns, and cheered triumphant heroes . . . and in street clothes, like everybody else, had undoubtedly driven cabs and slung hash and loved their children and hated their in-laws when they got home . . .

She'd see them every morning on arrival, lined up outside Belle Delaney's office just within the studio gates: *'You got anything for me today, Belle?'* If the answer was no, it was a short streetcar ride down Sunset Boulevard to Nestor or Enterprise or Monarch, hoping for that three dollars and fifty cents that might prove the difference between making the rent and packing your slender belongings in a shoebox and doing a midnight flit.

'So charge in there like you mean it!' Madge flung fisted hands into the air like a Ruritanian dictator yelling for the head of the hero.

Four dollars, Emma thought, if you were a 'dress extra' in a rich-people's party scene and you had your own evening dress.

Five-fifty, for those displaced cowboys who'd drifted West with the closing of the cattle ranges, to become 'riding extras'. Most of these, Emma knew, were at this moment over in Wardrobe, being fitted by Millie Katz in cavalry uniforms while the studio wrangler and the fellow from Chatsworth Livery out in the San Fernando Valley saddled up a 150 horses . . .

Mr Madison will never track down all the extras.

She lowered the newspaper and frowned, completely ignoring the sudden near-riot as forty-two enraged citizens of Rome burst the gates of the Babylonian empress's garden to surround poor Darlene Golden, cowering at Kitty's feet. Though the film was silent, the mob cried, 'Slay her! Slay her!' though several gentlemen audibly yelled, 'Repeal Prohibition!'

An extra could walk all over the lot in costume and nobody would look twice at him.

Emma got to her feet and went back into Stage One, threading her way between the empress's deserted balcony, where it was still night (with the stars dark in the backdrop of the sky) and a vaguely Regency parlor being set up for a party sequence in *Scandalous Lady*, and so to the outer door. From it the Hacienda was visible, across the dusty plaza bounded by the studio gates, and, extending from one side of the Hacienda, the dressing rooms.

People crossed and recrossed the square: extras in swanky evening dress, prop-men carrying chairs. Young women from the accounting and purchasing offices wearing the short skirts that Emma still found slightly disconcerting. (Her mother, she recalled, had been scandalized at the three inches of leg visible above Emma's ankle in her VAD uniform. What she'd say of the current hemlines – just below the knee . . .!) A trickle of cameramen, of shirtsleeved gaffers and drivers emerged from the canteen, where Mr Madison was still hard at work.

The thought of Gloria Swanson or Peggy Donovan murdering a rival in order to win a *Screen Stories* contest – additional picture or not – was almost, but not completely, ridiculous on the face of it. Someone like Theda Bara – a sultry vamp now pushing forty, according to Zal, who hadn't made a picture for nearly five years – might conceivably think it a good idea, especially if she regarded Camille de la Rose as her only real competition.

But Camille de la Rose – even without the cachet of being arrested for a crime of passion – *wasn't* the only competition.

And an actress who had even a chance of being named the Goddess of the Silver Screen would presumably have the money to hire someone to do the job for her. (*How much do assassins charge in Los Angeles these days? I wonder if Mr Madison knows?*) Would one of them be so silly as not to realize that an accomplice would blackmail her?

Baroque scenarios of Gloria Swanson taking a murderer for her lover and then shooting him herself (*What would she do with the body?*) flitted briefly through Emma's mind . . . *I think I've been in Hollywood too long . . .*

Peggy Donovan – the red-haired hot tomato over at Enterprise who was Kitty's bosom friend – would probably consider that a perfectly reasonable plan.

And it did occur to her to save the idea for a future scenario . . .

Now I KNOW I've been in Hollywood too long . . .

Emma sighed, and crossed to the small side-door of the Hacienda which opened into the studio telephone exchange.

Vinnie Lowder – very young, very stout, her blonde hair screwed into a wispy pompadour and a look of cornered anxiety in her lovely blue eyes – sat at her switchboard, trying to read another copy of the *Herald* but, Emma thought, not able to concentrate. The girl looked up quickly and said, 'Oh, Mrs Blackstone! I'm so sorry about what I said to that police detective—'

'Was it true?' Emma took one of the room's wooden desk chairs and spoke in her gentlest voice, as if calming a shopgirl who'd just spilled nail varnish all over a customer. 'Of course you had to speak the truth, and it's a good thing that you did!

I think even Mr Pugh will see that, once he calms down. Think what a horrid mess there'd be, if you came up with a lie and they caught you in it – which they would, you know. Then everything would look even worse.'

'That's what I thought!' Vinnie's rosebud mouth puckered briefly, in an effort not to cry. 'I mean, I didn't exactly think it at that moment, but I've always felt that. That if you tell a lie and get found out, it always makes things more complicated. But Ginny Field – she was outside Mr Thaxter's dressing room – says she heard Mr Pugh say he was going to f-fire me . . .' She almost couldn't get the words out.

'I'll speak to Mr Pugh,' said Emma. 'And I'll tell Miss de la Rose to speak to him as well. You know he'll listen to her.'

The girl nodded, desperate for reassurance. The switchboard buzzed at that point and she quickly plugged in a wire, saying into her speaking-tube, 'Foremost Productions . . . Yes, Mr Goldwyn, I'll connect you . . .'

She changed over the wire. 'Thank you,' she said simply. 'I just *can't* lose this job. People always want to know why . . .'

'You won't.' Emma leaned a little forward. 'What time did that call come in?'

'Ten minutes after two,' replied the girl promptly. 'A man called, asking for Miss de la Rose. When I connected to her phone, a man's voice answered in her dressing room.' She looked a little self-conscious. 'Which doesn't mean anything, you know, Mrs Blackstone. It could have been Mr Volmort from Make-Up, or someone sent over to fetch something from the set, you know.'

Actually, Emma was well aware that in Kitty's case, a man in Kitty's dressing room often *did* mean something, but not, as a general rule, in the middle of the day. Unless he was very good-looking . . . or Kitty had had a bit more gin than usual . . .

But it took a good deal of gin to make Kitty that careless (or the man in question had to be *extremely* comely), and in general, she answered her own telephone.

'The man said, "Yes, she's right here", and then, "Camille, come to the phone".'

'He called her Camille? You're sure?'

'Oh, yes. I didn't think anything about it at the time, but

would her former husband call her Camille and not Kitty?
Though I suppose if they've been separated for so long . . .'

Like pretty much everyone at Foremost, Vinnie was under
the impression that Camille was Kitty's real name.

'And you didn't hear Miss de la Rose's reply?'

'Oh, no. I disconnected myself from the call at once.' She
blushed a little. 'I know better than that. Even when . . . well,
certain people . . . would pay me to listen, it wouldn't make
up for losing a steady job.'

Thelma Turnbit, presumably . . . and a dozen like her.

'And you didn't recognize the caller's voice? Or that of the
man who answered?'

Vinnie shook her head. 'The man who answered would
have to have been poor Mr Festraw, wouldn't he? Wasn't that
awful, what the newspaper said he did to her? I never knew
– she's *so* brave . . . I didn't know the caller's voice. It wasn't
one I've heard a lot – or at all, probably.'

'Young man's voice? Old man's?'

'A regular man,' said the girl, after a moment's thought.
'Not a boy, and not creaky like a very old man gets. Sort of
light – not deep like Mr Pugh's – and well-spoken. No accent,
I mean, and – well – upper-class. Like someone with an education. But of course he only asked me to connect to Miss de
la Rose's dressing room . . .'

'Of course,' said Emma, recalling Taffy the Bootlegger's
slangy New York patois. 'Thank you. It doesn't sound like
anyone Miss de la Rose knows, or at least not anyone I've
met. I promise I'll tell Miss de la Rose to speak to Mr Pugh,
and to Mr Fishbein, but I don't really think you have anything
to worry about . . .'

The switchboard buzzed again and Vinnie plugged in
another wire. 'Foremost Productions. Oh, yes, Mrs Pugh. I'll
connect you right away. But I know Mr Pugh is away on
location this morning—'

Emma had seen him ten minutes previously, crossing from
the canteen to the Hacienda.

'Of course. Of course . . .'

Thoughtfully – as yet another line buzzed – she waved her
farewell with a smile, which Vinnie returned, and took her leave.

She stood for a moment outside the door, watching as the property men carried armloads of costumes, shoes, kimonos, gramophone records, and wicker dog beds up the outside steps to the shaded gallery along the upper floor of dressing rooms. A wrangler passed across the square, leading four horses in what Hollywood fondly believed to be Roman saddles (meaning blankets strapped over English saddles, with anachronistic stirrups visibly dangling).

Father would turn in his grave.

A man emerged from Kitty's door bearing Ambrose Crain's silver vase of crimson roses, blown-out now and beginning to shed their petals. These strewed the steps behind him as he climbed, like a trail of dripped blood on the stairs.

SEVEN

The canteen was still full of people.

Only a few of them – guards, drivers, Darlene Golden's stand-in Evvie Parton, a little crone whom Emma recognized as one of Mary Blanque's seamstresses from Wardrobe – weren't glancing irritably at their watches and then at the little cubicle of screens. Emma was surprised at how many of the people in the line she knew, at least by name. Even some of the extras – Ricardo Diaz from Spring Street downtown, who had a face like a sixteenth-century buccaneer, and Peachy Blume, as always resplendent in an evening gown sufficiently elegant to get her hired but not eye-catching enough to compete with the star in any scene – 'Heya, Duchess, you going by Stage Two? Would you be a doll and tell Larry I'm still sittin' in the *verkakte* line? Bless you, sweetheart . . .'

Emma stepped around the screens just as Sam Wyatt, the studio's regular scenarist, was saying, 'Where was I? I was behind my desk where I'd been since eight o'clock yesterday morning and where I was until midnight last night, tryin' to come up with some kind of endin' for that bag of sugar-coated moonshine they're filmin' over on Stage Two, is where I was, and if Larry comes bangin' on my door this afternoon askin' where the hell is scene eighty-five, I'm gonna refer him to you, buster . . .'

'Yeah?' Madison's chin came forward. 'So when the LAPD hauls Miss de la Rose away in handcuffs and the studio closes and everybody, including yourself, are out of a job, and they come to ask me how come? I'm gonna refer them to *you*.'

Drunk, Sam Wyatt's responses to self-important provocation were legendary – and Emma saw the shy little secretary that Fishbein had lent Madison getting ready to bolt. But Sam only rolled his eyes, shook out a smoke from his pocket, and said in a patient voice, 'At one fifteen yesterday I was at my desk working, and I was there until I heard the commotion and the cops downstairs. After they all went away I went back to work. I didn't go to the windows, I didn't hear a shot. Nuthin'.'

He even ignored Madison's smug nod of triumph, as if the refusal to get into a quarrel over the matter were an act of cowardice. When the detective said, 'You got that, kid?' to the secretary, Sam picked up his hat and quietly departed.

'Yeah, beautiful.' This to Emma. 'What can I do you for?' He had very bright, very lazy blue eyes under dark lashes which contrasted strikingly with that corn-silk hair. A short, straight nose and a mouth made for kisses, at present occupied by most of a cigarette. His glance was an invitation: *I can have you for the asking, baby, and you'll beg me for more.*

Emma wanted to pour the secretary's tumbler of water over his head.

'I won't keep you but a moment,' promised Emma, stepping aside to let Sam past her. 'You wouldn't happen to have made a note of Mr Festraw's address, would you?'

'You bet I did.' He fished in the pocket of his wide-lapelled jacket and produced a notebook. 'But I warn you, honey, the bulls went through that place like Sherman going through Georgia and I doubt you'll find so much as a laundry ticket there now.'

'It can't hurt to have a look. Is this his telephone number?' Just above the address – 202 East Third Street, # 4H – was a string of letters and numbers: MI 59063.

'You ain't planning on going down there, are you, doll? 'Cause I'll bet you, that hotel – the Winterdon – has already got that room cleaned out, hosed down, and rented to some other sucker. The phone number's Frannie's, a deli over on Flower. Good pastrami.'

He shrugged, and gave her another visual once-over, as if adding up the pale-brown silk of her old-fashioned bun, the neat challis skirt and plain shirtwaist. 'You're Camille's . . . secretary? Don't tell me you're her sister . . .' He was clearly comparing her height and long-legged slenderness with Kitty's pocket-Venus sensuality.

'Sister-in-law.' Emma held out her hand. 'Mrs Blackstone.'

He grasped it, firm, warm fingers and, she noticed, manicured nails. 'I understand you wanting to help, sis,' he said.

'Frank tells me she fished you out of some pretty grim bouil-
labaisse in Blighty. But I have an instinct about these things,
and this stinks of politics. Anything aimed at the studios does.'
    'You don't think it would be worthwhile to try to find out
a little more about Mr Festraw?'
    His grin was engagingly boyish. 'Don't tell me you believe
Fishbein's applesauce about bootleggers! No, baby, it's
pretty clear to me Festraw came to town to put the touch
on Camille, and somebody in City Hall – or the police –
heard about it and followed him to the studio, hoping to
touch off a scandal that would look real good on their record,
come election time. Studios are always big news. Camille
de la Rose – the Goddess of the Silver Screen, the Queen
of "It".' His hands framed an imaginary movie screen. 'What
more could any crooked cop want?'
    Emma parted her lips to object that this view took no account
of the phone call – at precisely the moment to establish that
Kitty was in her dressing room with Rex – but Colt Madison
patted her hand with another dazzling display of perfect teeth.
    'If you want my advice, sugar, don't get yourself mixed up
with this. I know what I'm doing. I've dealt with these goons
for years. Unless' – his blue eyes got suddenly sharp – 'you
know something about where Camille really *was* between two
and four?'
    Emma made a swift decision, withdrew her hand from his,
and widened her eyes. 'I think she was in the backlot, looking
for her dog.'

Filming would go on, she knew, for as long as daylight lasted;
it was barely nine fifteen. After Mr Madison's cloying caresses
her first urge was to go wash her hands, but as she stepped
around the screen she was intercepted by Sam Wyatt, a thin
sheaf of scenario pages in his hand. 'Say, Mrs B, you wouldn't
know why snooty rich ladies fire their maids, would you? I
mean unfairly – this girl ain't no thief or nuthin'.' He gestured
with the pages. Medium-sized, dark, and thin, Sam Wyatt had
run guns to the Arabs in the War, driven a taxicab in El Paso
and operated a saloon on Zanzibar. Nevertheless, he frequently
came to Emma to double-check the likely behavior of the

wealthy aristocrats about whom he was required to write tales, as if they were inhabitants of an alien planet.

'Spilling perfume,' said Emma promptly, remembering Mrs Pendergast. 'Accused of stealing something that's been mislaid. Or if Mrs Snooty has a son of marriageable age who tries to kiss the poor girl, or thinks she's beautiful, that would do it. Is East Third Street in Los Angeles a decent neighborhood?' she inquired, into Sam's expression of shocked outrage. 'I mean, safe for a woman to go to alone?'

'Oh, sure, sure. I mean, it's not fancy – it's just a street, you know. You'll be plenty safe, unless you step in front of a taxi or somethin'.'

'And are you familiar with a delicatessen called Frannie's? On Flower Street?'

'Yeah, Eighth and Flower.' He thumbed his scenario pages to find one so scribbled-over as to be useless, then fished a pencil from his pocket and sketched a map. 'For a buck they'll sell you some of the worst bootleg tonsil-varnish I've ever got drunk on, out the back door. Good pastrami.'

Armed with these reassurances, Emma took the bright yellow streetcar along Sunset Boulevard, and thence down Broadway into Los Angeles itself. Big frame houses nestled in the sunlight on hillsides behind St Vincent's Hospital; the slopes bright with white and golden wildflowers against the dusty-gray background of brush that had made the town look so dreary when she'd arrived with Kitty last Fall. Here and there weird plants punctuated the general sage, fleshy leaves with spiky tips, or weird clusters of things like sword blades, more suited to Mr Burroughs' Barsoom than to Earth. Leaving England, Emma had known she would miss the beech and oak and ivy of the woods . . . but hadn't been prepared for this outré otherworld flora.

Any more, she reflected, than she'd been prepared for Chinese and Mexican food.

As the Yellow Car approached the hills of the city's center, more and more dilapidated adobe structures appeared, amid the stretches of weeds and cactus. Then rather grim brick apartment buildings and residence hotels, and automobiles that blocked the streetcar's progress at every intersection under a thickening spiderweb of telephone and electrical wires overhead.

At one such delay, Emma consulted Sam Wyatt's sketch-map, to see how far it was from the Winterdon to Frannie's, and was momentarily distracted by the strong, black scribble of titles, names, and cryptic plot-notes on the back.

> Stop the Clock. Kentucky Derby Katie. Turn Back the
> ~~Clock. Time~~. Years. Cash or Check? The Monkey's
> Eyebrows.
> ~~Ellie McCall~~. Goldie ~~McCall~~ M'Gurk. Blind Pig M'Gurk.
> ~~Hammie~~ Blackie Denham
> Ted tries to stay away (Blackie threatens)?
> Building burns, Ellie disappears (?)
> Amnesia – marries Roger
> Kidnapped – switches clothes with maid – secret
> love-child
> Oscar finds

Who's Oscar? Emma wondered. And what happened to Ted?

> Sinister Chinaman pursuing Goldie – really father's
> servant – twins
> Higginbotham murdered, ~~father~~ Roger accused

As the streetcar lurched into motion again, Emma lowered the paper and wondered what any of the stirring events hinted at had to do with a monkey's eyebrows. As the buildings around her grew taller and grimier, she pushed aside the uncomfortable sensation behind her breastbone, and told herself firmly not to be silly. London was a *much* larger city than Los Angeles, and presumably a more dangerous one, with its crowded tenements, concealing fogs, and miles of dockside flophouses . . .

But I KNOW London.

She had trodden London's sidewalks a thousand times: with her father, from Paddington to the British Museum; with her mother or Aunt Margaret to their dressmaker on Jermyn Street or to the Regent's Arcade. With her family, via Underground, to Kensington, to marvel at the great, gray, threatening shapes of the dinosaurs outside the Crystal Palace . . .

Los Angeles, with its surreal palm trees and grubby gray-green weeds growing through the cracks of every sidewalk, with its brown faces and black faces mingling with the white, its glaring billboards (*What on EARTH does a candy bar have to do with playing baseball . . .?*), was an alien place.

Hot, dusty, and threatening.

Ante omnia tempus habent, she told herself firmly. *There is a first time for all things.* The Winterdon Hotel on Third Street was, a little to Emma's surprise, not the sordid flophouse she had extrapolated from Rex Festraw's seedy coat and liquor-laden breath. It was a four-story brick building stuccoed white, its shallow porch flanked by bougainvillea bushes already gorgeous with magenta flowers. The lobby, when she climbed its three low steps, though starkly plain, was spotless and smelled of bleach. The leather couch and chairs were old but in good repair. The middle-aged man behind the counter – backed by a wall divided equally between keys and pigeonholes for mail – was clean, prim-faced, clearly sober, and redolent of soap and piety.

Mr Festraw must have had more money than he appeared, if he was staying here.

She said, 'Excuse me,' and approached the counter. Halfway down from Hollywood she'd realized her name may have appeared in Thelma Turnbit's column as Kitty's 'secretary and companion', and though this gentleman didn't look as if he'd touched a film magazine in his life, she recalled what Zal had said last night. It was better to be safe than sorry. 'My name is Flavian – Mrs Augustus Flavian. Is this . . .? Did a man named Rex Festraw stay here?'

The clerk's upper lip lengthened and his thin nostrils flared. 'He did, m'am.' His gentle drawl marked him as a transplant from the American South. 'I'm afraid he is no longer a resident.'

Whatever grief he felt about this could have been concealed behind a folded gum-wrapper.

'No,' said Emma. 'No, I understand he . . . He's deceased. Under unfortunate circumstances.'

The clerk's chill eye spoke of un-Christian thoughts, piously suppressed.

'The thing is,' she went on, 'I'm looking for . . . that is, Mr Festraw . . .' She puckered her brow and clutched the clasp of her handbag in what she hoped sufficiently resembled distress. Kitty had told her once about imagining herself in her characters' situations (though Emma would have been hard-pressed to guess her own reactions had she actually found herself Empress of Babylon . . .). 'My sister became – involved – with Mr Festraw just before Christmas. She left home – she's only seventeen, and . . . She's very good-hearted,' she added earnestly. 'But . . . wild. Impulsive. We got a postcard that she'd left with Mr Festraw, but we've only just heard – my mother and I – that they came here to Los Angeles. Did Mr Festraw . . . was there a woman . . . a girl, really . . .'

'Mr Festraw' – the clerk handled the name as he would have handled a deceased mouse discovered in his soup – 'generally did not spend his evenings here at the Winterdon. The woman he brought here this past Monday night' – he looked Emma up and down with eyes like ball bearings – 'would not have been any relation to a lady such as yourself, m'am.'

Emma lowered her eyes and tried to picture a maenad like the Emperor Augustus' wastrel daughter Julia, clinging to Rex Festraw's arm. In a subdued voice, she murmured, 'What did she look like, sir? Julia . . .' She stopped herself, as if too mortified to go on.

'She is shorter than yourself, m'am,' said the clerk, in the tone of one washing his hands of the whole encounter. 'And . . . ahem . . . voluptuously built. Her hair is red – rather emphatically so – bobbed short and waved.' He paused to consider, approvingly, the braided knot at the back of Emma's neck, and the hemline that Kitty had more than once informed her 'went out with bustles'. 'She wore a frock of red artificial silk flowered in black and her fingernails looked like she'd started to grow them long before Christmastime. They were painted, too. Quite vivid red.' More gently, he added, 'She didn't look seventeen, m'am, or anywhere near it. And her speech, when she opened her mouth, was nothing like yours.'

And, when Emma said nothing, he went on, 'I'm sorry.'

'And Mr Festraw never mentioned any other . . . any other companion?'

'I never had words with the man.' The chilly eyes softened to kindness. 'He arrived last Thursday night, just a week ago. His room had been paid for in advance. He had only a small suitcase with him, and the police removed that yesterday when they came. He only slept here, but he'd come in late some nights – walking steady, but I could smell the liquor on him, from where I stood here behind the counter. Monday night was the only night he brought a woman here, and I don't need to tell you, that of course I didn't let her past the lobby.'

The narrow lips tightened again. 'I asked her to leave – in my opinion she was also intoxicated – and she did. Then ten minutes later I had to stop Mr Festraw from unlocking the rear service door of the hotel which opens into the alley. Had Mr Festraw not met with an unfortunate accident yesterday, I would probably have asked that he take his custom to another establishment. He was not the sort of guest we look for here at the Winterdon.'

Emma looked around her at the lobby and exclaimed, 'Oh, heavens, no!' Then she frowned again, as if puzzled, and said, 'His room was paid for in advance? *De mortuis nihil nisi bonum*, of course, but that hardly sounds like what I know of Mr Festraw.'

'I am of one mind with you on that head, m'am. But it might help you to get in touch with this' – he opened a drawer under the counter, removed a blue-backed ledger, and looked up a notation – '*Mr Stanislas Markham* in New York, who might be able to give you some further clues about Mr Festraw's other acquaintances in Los Angeles. That might point you in the direction of finding word of your sister.'

Emma gasped, 'Oh!' Her face flooded with unfeigned delight. She hadn't hoped for any information so definite as a name. 'Oh, sir, I cannot thank you enough! God bless you, sir! I can never repay your kindness!'

And she made a note of the name, shook hands with the clerk, and hurried out the door, reflecting that writing improbable scenarios for Foremost Productions appeared to provide valuable training after all.

She was seriously tempted to return to the studio at that point. *Who on EARTH is Stanislas Markham of New York and WHY would he pay for a hotel room for Mr Festraw . . . And did the police think to ask about this?* But the mild brightness of the spring day, and her unexpected success, gave her heart. After consulting the correct side of Sam Wyatt's sketch-map, Emma walked the some twelve blocks, past the trees and fountain of Pershing Square and up the tidy, downtown streets to Frannie's Delicatessen, at Eighth Street and Flower.

The large room with its black-and-white tile floor was a little grimier than the Winterdon, and very much more noisy. The entire place seemed to be tiled, without a soft surface anywhere to be seen, save the bodies and clothing of the people seated at the tiny, marble-topped, round tables. Their voices ricocheted from walls, floor, and pressed-copper ceiling like an avalanche of ping-pong balls: gentlemen in business suits whose condition and cleanliness advertised the wearer's probable financial state; women in neat frocks like the ladies of Wardrobe or Vinnie Lowder; ladies in outrageously short skirts or fringed frocks with no sleeves. Dusky Mexican mothers helped black-haired, black-eyed children eat ice-cream sodas. A black girl of sixteen or so, neatly dressed as for work in an office, hurried in, waved a quick greeting to the young man behind the counter and made straight for the three telephone boxes just beyond the end of the counter itself. She dropped in her coin without closing the booth door, dialed, and had a hasty conversation – no more than a sentence or two – before hanging up.

Then she crossed back to the counter, asked the young man, 'Anybody call for me, Roy?'

He fished a slip of paper from his shirt pocket and pushed it across to her. 'Sounded like your sister. She just asked you to call.'

The girl glanced at the number and beamed like a reprieved life prisoner. 'God bless you, Roy. Coffee and a donut?' While Roy was getting them she went straight back to the telephone

box. The young man – red-haired and freckled from hairline
to collarbone – set the coffee and sweet, together with a paper
napkin, at the end of the counter for her, and turned with a
welcoming smile as Emma approached.

'Can I help you, m'am?'

Emma glanced at the girl in the phone box – the second
box was now occupied by a slender dark gentleman in the
overalls of a petrol-station attendant – and said, 'I'm looking
for a woman who I think uses your telephone to make her
calls. Do you have tea?' She sat on one of the tall, leatherette-
cushioned stools. 'And that donut smells awfully good.' It was
no flattery; the pastry on its thick white porcelain plate waiting
for the girl in the phone box glistened with freshness and
glaze. 'Might I have one also?'

''Fraid we don't have tea, m'am.' Roy tonged a donut from
some mysterious bin below the counter. Even his arms and
hands were freckled. 'Just brewed a new pot of coffee, though.
As for the lady you're lookin' for, I guess half the neighborhood uses this place as an office and me as the secretary . . .'
He grinned, as, at her assent, he poured out some coffee and
gently pushed the cream pitcher and sugar jar in her direction.
In a stage whisper, he added, 'Least I don't have to wear a
frilly hat an' high-heeled shoes!'

Emma's eyes twinkled back at him. 'Oh, I don't know; I
think one of those fascinators with a couple of long feathers
would suit the shape of your face very well.'

'I been told I should never wear an eye-veil,' he returned,
in mock anxiety.

'Whoever told you that was simply jealous of your cheekbones. It would be quite becoming.'

'It would be coming off.' His grin widened. 'What's she
look like, this lady? I know pretty much all the regulars.'

Emma repeated the description the clerk at the Winterdon
had given her, and saw the bright, bantering look fade from
the counterman's lashless green eyes. 'Well,' he said. 'Her.'

And he studied Emma in silence for a moment.

'I'm not a bill collector,' said Emma quietly. 'Nor with the
police. I just . . . She knows – knew – an acquaintance of
mine, who met with an accident yesterday. I'm trying to find

out what he was doing in Los Angeles, and who else he might
have known in town. He was . . .' She hesitated, looking aside
a little shamefacedly, trying to imagine Lesbia asking Catullus
for money. 'He was supposed to be bringing my mother money.'

'If he was keepin' company with Phyllis,' said the counterman, his voice suddenly dry, 'I'm sorry to tell you, m'am,
that he likely wouldn't have a dime of your mama's money
left in his pockets.'

Emma conjured all the resources of her imagination, and
murmured, 'Thank you. I still have to try.'

''Course.' He nodded towards the plate-glass window,
which gave a view, across the brightness of Flower Street, of
a four-story building in yellowish brick, like a cardboard box
whose corners were capped with unlikely-looking square
turrets. 'She lives someplace in there.' He glanced at the
clock, just beside the telephone boxes. 'She ain't been in yet,
and she usually comes in for coffee an' to make phone calls,
oh, close to noon. She'll be in an' I think' – his eyes narrowed,
calculating – 'she'll be awake. Phyllis Blossom. Does extra
work – she says – over at Century . . . when she's sober.'

He turned away then, and went to take the order of a couple
of uniformed policemen a few seats down the counter. Emma
sipped her coffee – which when sufficiently doctored with
cream and sugar bordered on drinkable – and turned over in
her mind what Roy had said, and what she had learned, over
the past few months, about young ladies who claimed to work
'in the pictures' who didn't get much work. It was – she turned
to look at the clock – eleven fifteen. At the studio they would
be midway through scene ten. She supposed she could wait
in Frannie's until Miss Blossom came in . . . *if* Miss Blossom
came in.

When Roy next had a moment to spare he brought her a
slip with the price of her refreshment scribbled on it – twenty-
five cents – and she laid thirty-five on top of the little paper.
Leaving her handbag slightly open and nudging a one-dollar
bill far enough out of it to show, she looked into the young
man's eyes and said, 'You're going to think this terribly forward
of me – Mother would die of mortification if she thought I'd
gone to . . . well, to certain lengths to get information from

the sort of woman it sounds like this Miss Blossom is . . . But would you know of any . . . any *argument* that might gain me her time and attention for a few minutes? That would keep her from shutting the door in my face?'

The young counterman's eyes moved from her face to her handbag, then back up again to her face, on which she wore an expression which she hoped would convey forlorn embarrassment and desperation. Like Juliet: *Come weep with me, past hope, past cure, past help* . . .

After a moment's struggle with himself he said, 'Go down to the corner of Ninth and around to the alley. Our back door's the third one along. Knock twice.'

Wishing she could blush on cue – her cousin Maud could – she looked away from him, lips pursed as if in great pain (*Mother really WOULD die of mortification* . . . And the recollection, even at four years' distance, that her mother *had* actually died brought genuine tears to her eyes). She managed to whisper, 'Thank you,' and slid the bill under the donut plate as she slipped from the stool, and hastened out the door.

EIGHT

B reathless as she was at her own shame and embarrassment (*Aunt Margaret was right when she said bad
company would turn a woman bad . . .*), Emma had to
admit that the little brown bottle that Roy passed to her through
the back door of Frannie's worked like a miracle. It was un-
labeled, but strong enough – when, in Phyllis Blossom's grubby
furnished room, she unscrewed it to add to the reheated coffee
that the 'actress' poured out for them both – to fell a horse.

Miss Blossom shut her eyes and sighed after the first long
swig, like a woman warmed to the ends of her red-nailed toes.
'Shit fuck, I needed that. You are a fucking angel, Mrs F.'

'Um . . . Thank you.' By her tone, Miss Blossom was obviously sincere.

The excuse Emma gave for the liquor – and for her visit
– was to let Miss Phyllis Blossom know that Rex Festraw had
'met with an accident', and to offer her sympathy and solace.
At the news Miss Blossom voiced a string of curses in a tone
that held no anger, nor even sorrow: just a sort of philosophical
melancholy at the shortness of men's days. 'The Corneros get
him?' she asked, curious rather than vengeful.

'Who?'

'Tony the Hat, and his brother Frank. Biggest rum-runners
in town. They bring in the stuff by freighters from Canada,
unload it into motorboats to bring it ashore at Long Beach
and then truck it into the clubs. I told Rex not to get mixed
up with those guys.'

Good Heavens, was Mr Fishbein right after all?

'I didn't think Mr Festraw was in Los Angeles long enough
to even meet bootleggers,' said Emma, and Miss Blossom,
with an absent-minded air, took the bottle and dumped about
a gill of it into her half-empty coffee cup.

'Oh, Rex was connected.' She made a long arm for her
bright-red handbag, perched on a corner of the minuscule table

on top of a litter of bills, magazines, bread-wrappers and stray items of tableware, and extracted a cigarette. 'He worked for Joe Adonis and the Luciano boys in New York. He said he was out here on other business, but needed some extra.' Miss Blossom shook her head, and lit the little tube of tobacco. As the clerk at the Winterdon had promised, her fingernails were long, red as sealing-wax, and chipped.

Familiar as Emma was, after six months in Hollywood, with cosmetic embellishment that would have gotten any girl she'd previously known thrown into the street, Phyllis Blossom redefined the limits of the vulgar. At least, Emma reflected, her highly-painted sister-in-law knew how to apply her make-up. The blood-crimson of Miss Blossom's lips made Kitty's efforts in that direction look virginal. Her small, rather puffy, hazel eyes glinted from caked masses of kohl and rouge, and her mascaro looked as if she'd slept in it, and then simply applied a fresh coat on top of last night's.

She had, in fact, upon Emma's arrival at her door, been dressing to go out. Curling tongs lay across an unwashed frying pan on the room's single gas ring: the tiny apartment smelled of scorched styling lotion and lightly charred hair.

'I never saw a man unload as much as Rex did, on the ponies, and the fights – I swear if he'd lived long enough for baseball to start he'd have been in the poorhouse.' She shook her head sadly. 'He sure knew how to show a girl a good time, but he couldn't have picked the winner in a fight between a lion and ham sandwich. When he showed up Monday throwin' money around like confetti – and I knew he'd done a job for Tony Cornero Friday, soon as he got into town – I said, "You better be careful messin' around with them boys".

'You know what he said? He said, "Relax, doll. I don't have to make the drop to Tony 'til Friday, and with the dough I got comin' in Wednesday, he won't even know it's gone".'

'And he never mentioned what money he had coming in on Wednesday?'

Miss Blossom shook her head, shrugged, and removed her cigarette long enough to drain her now cold coffee cocktail. Emma couldn't imagine how she swallowed the stuff. Her own cup was untouched. The liquid smelled like motor oil, and whatever it was in Roy's bottle couldn't have helped. 'Guys like Rex, they always got money comin' in. Or say they do.'

'Did he mention who else he might have seen or spoken to here in town?'

'Well, Tony and Frank. And somebody named Al, who he said was a cheap-ass Jew-bastard and didn't pay worth shit, and somebody else named Sid, who was fucking worthless as far as Rex was concerned and was never around when you needed to get hold of him, and somebody else named Jerry, who Rex said would . . . well, it doesn't matter 'cause it's just what men say about other men they don't like. It didn't sound like it had anything to do with your mama's money. I'm sure sorry, honey.'

Miss Blossom leaned across the corner of the cluttered table and patted Emma's hand. 'I swear to you, if Rex had any plans to hand over so much as a dollar to your poor mother, he didn't act like it. I can't even really say I'm sorry he's dead, because he was a real dick when he was drunk, but I'm sorry you and your mama got screwed.'

'It's all right.' Emma manufactured a brave smile, trying to look as if it wasn't. Then she frowned, and added, as an afterthought, 'He didn't happen to mention his ex-wife, did he? Or his wife, he might have called her – someone named Kitty?'

It crossed her mind then how he'd pronounced *de la Rose* in the stage. Almost mockingly. And he had known her as Kitty, the name she'd gone by as a chorus dancer on Broadway. Yet the man Vinnie had heard on the telephone had called her Camille. Would Rex have countered that with, *You mean Kitty?*

The young woman's eyes narrowed as she cast her mind back. 'I don't think so,' she said. ''Course, that kind of guy, he's not gonna breathe a word about an ex-wife to the girl he's seein', much less a wife. Crap,' she added, glancing at the new – and very expensive-looking – watch that adorned her slender wrist. 'I gotta go, or I'm gonna be late. Look,' she said, as she and Emma stood. 'You need money? You OK for carfare, and a place to stay . . .?'

She reached for her handbag again.

'Really,' said Emma, startled, 'I'm quite all right.'

'You sure?' She'd pulled a five-dollar bill from the bag. 'It's no skin off my ass, it's Rex's money, so you got it comin'.'

After a panic-stricken moment as she tried to decide what her assumed persona of a robbed woman would have done, Emma looked shamefaced again (*And you SHOULD be ashamed . . .!*) and held out her hand. 'Thank you,' she said. 'You're very kind.'

As she stepped out into the hallway she glanced back, to see Miss Blossom swig down the remainder of the bottle – which Emma had left on the table – and then the contents of Emma's cold and untouched coffee cup.

Well, I suppose if Odysseus could get information by giving libations to the spirits in Hell, it's no surprise it works here as well.

She took the streetcar back to the studio.

'Sounds like the cops never even got in touch with her,' Zal remarked, when, many hours later, he joined Emma in Kitty's little base-camp with the usual half-dozen paper cartons of chow mein and egg fu yung for a late and hasty dinner before embarking on scene fifty-three. Chairs, make-up table, folding rack of kimonos, gramophone, dogs, pillows and magazine bin had all been carried to the same corner of Stage One in which they'd been set up yesterday (*Was it ONLY yesterday?*). Kitty had slipped away immediately after scene seventy-seven (the Empress Valerna's confrontation with Nero). 'Darling, you *will* look after my tiny beloveds for me, won't you?'

Emma wondered if it was the same man this time, or a different one. Or Frank Pugh, who was on the lot that day . . .

Darlene Golden had certainly been looking daggers at her all through rehearsals, walk-through, and setting up the lights for the virtuous Philomela's plea for the lives of her co-religionists.

The virtuous Philomela was still out in the shadows of the empress's garden, sitting on the pedestal of the *Rape of the Sabine Women* (the original sculpted in 1583 and almost certainly not a part of Nero's palace décor), deep in conversation with a good-looking young man in a tuxedo. Kitty's stand-in Ginny Field joined them, the young man – clearly a refugee from the Ruritanian palace ball taking place (still) that day on Stage Two – producing a hip flask. Beside Emma's chair, Chang Ming and Black Jasmine, replete with dinner, snored in their boxes as only Pekinese can. As usual, Buttercreme had been too timid to eat, so Emma knew the little moonlight dog would need to be fed when they got back to the house up on Ivarene, at whatever hour *that* would be.

'*That home will be yours as well . . .*'

Emma pulled herself back to the present with an effort. 'I suspect Detective Meyer, like Mr Madison, has his own view of why Mr Festraw was killed, and isn't going to look in any other direction than that.'

'He may.' Zal set out little cartons of egg rolls and lo mein on the make-up table. 'Or he may not really give a rat's ass, and just wants to find some evidence damning enough that Pugh'll have to give him money to mislay it. Or,' he added generously, seeing Emma's exasperated expression, 'he may just be following orders about that from upstairs. A lot of 'em just do what they're told and don't ask why.'

Emma turned her face aside for a moment, feeling a little like Gulliver in Lilliput when confronted with the vicious internecine conflict over which end of the soft-boiled egg should be opened first. *After six months I shouldn't be bothered by this . . .*

But it was the first time she'd come up against it first-hand. And if anything went amiss at the special hearing, or at the trial . . .

'*That home will be yours as well . . .*'

'You should have seen the way Famous Players tried to smooth over Jack Barrymore pissing into the planters of the Plaza Hotel while he was filming *Jekyll and Hyde*.' Zal handed her a plate. 'If Rudy Valentino ever ran over a total stranger in broad daylight on Hollywood Boulevard, I'm pretty sure the nice folks at Ritz-Carlton Pictures would find some poor shlub in the studio to take the rap for him and do the time, so that Rudy could go on making money for them. That's Hollywood.'

Yes, thought Emma.

Did Odysseus feel this way, standing on the cliff-top of Ogygia, looking towards his home?

Slowly, she said, 'Someone paid for Rex Festraw to be in Los Angeles – obviously, for the purpose of murdering him in Kitty's dressing room. That's over a hundred dollars for even a third-class train ticket, not to speak of the cost of the room.'

'That's not actually a lot,' returned Zal, 'if he was acting as a runner for Luciano or Bugsy Siegel. Who knows what else he was really doing here in town? He may have used his connections here to try to put the touch on Kitty, like he said to your Miss Blossom, as a way of getting extra cash – in which case it would make sense for his New York employers to phone up Tony Cornero or somebody in the City Hall Gang and ask them to clean things up on their end. Putting the blame on Kitty would do exactly what it is doing: shoot off enough fireworks in the newspapers that nobody's going to look for who else might have wanted Festraw dead.'

Emma half-opened her mouth to reply, closed it, and went back over the things that bothered her, like potsherds laid out on a table in her father's study. *The probable impossible is to be preferred to the improbable possible . . .*

Behind them, voices echoed as the prop men and gaffers drifted in from the canteen again, to finish setting up the dungeon where the saintly but handsome Demetrius would resist being ravished by the Temptress of Babylon. It was nearly eight thirty: judging by the amount of set-up time needed, and a walk-through, and then close-ups, everyone was going to be on the set until midnight. *No wonder bootleggers peddle cocaine from the prop warehouse!*

'Maybe,' she said slowly. 'But . . . between the gun being stolen, and the stationery, and however they got Kitty away from the set at precisely the right time, I keep wondering if the real target isn't Kitty herself.'

Zal started to reply to that, but at that moment Madge yelled to him from the dungeon – something about having to shift the lights around – and he merely leaned over to give Emma a quick kiss, devoured a shrimp wonton, and hastened away, licking sauce from his fingers. At the same moment

Chang Ming and Black Jasmine woke, sat up, and began wagging their tails furiously, even Buttercreme ventured to poke her flat little nose around the edge of her basket doorway as Kitty slipped in through the huge rear doors from the moonlit garden.

'Don't be such a stick-in-the-mud, Ambrose!' she giggled, to the trim, elderly gentleman whom she tugged after her by the hand. 'I'll send Emma. Oh, there's Emma! Oh, and she's got Chinese food! I'll send Emma over to Wardrobe and we can get you fixed up as a Roman soldier – everybody's always sneaking their friends in as extras—'

'My entire family would disown me,' protested Ambrose Crain, chuckling. 'Or they would if they weren't so set on inheriting my shares in US Steel. And if the other members of the board of directors happened to see me in the background of a film they would suffer a collective seizure.'

'Chicken,' laughed Kitty. 'I double-dog dare you! And there, I told you I wouldn't be late! They're only just setting up the lights! Oh!' she added, picking up a pair of chopsticks. 'Oh, you darling, Emma, I have *absolutely* not had a *moment* to eat *anything* and I'm positively going to *faint* in front of the cameras. And anyway, we have to disguise poor Ambrose so Frank won't see him, when he comes in . . .'

'I'm flattered beyond words that you think I would blend in with the Roman legions, Kitten.' The old man caught, and kissed, her hand. 'But honestly, I will sit quietly in this corner and enjoy a cup of tea with Mrs Blackstone and watch you work . . . And trust me, I have the discretion to disappear when it becomes necessary. One cannot get you in dutch with the management.'

'Darling—' crooned Kitty, just as Madge bellowed from the set.

'Is that Kitty over there? Where the hell have you been? Somebody get Ginny in here!'

The lights went up with a hell-fire crackle and a blinding glare of bluish-green brilliance. Flinching and shading his eyes, Mr Crain took the folding chair at Emma's side. He wasn't the only audience, lingering in the shadows around the dungeon set: Emma glimpsed, beside the doorway that led out to the empress's garden, both Darlene Golden and the handsome young man in the tuxedo giggling now uncontrollably. Ginny Field scampered past them, at a distance eerily identical to Kitty in her diaphanous golden gauze and ersatz rubies, the dark cloud of her hair sparkling with gems. From another direction Scotty Sears ambled in, the middle-aged stand-in for the handsome young star Ken Elmore, shedding his bathrobe to reveal muscles glistening with cocoa butter and a loincloth the size of a business envelope.

Beside Emma, Mr Crain murmured, 'Extraordinary,' as Madge ordered Scotty and Ginny to take their places in front of the new arrangement of the lights so that Zal could adjust his lenses.

'Emma, darling . . .' Kitty came hurrying back to them. 'There's some champagne in my dressing room . . . the new dressing room, upstairs . . . or see if Margaret over on Stage Two has some cognac . . . Margaret always has cognac in her handbag . . .'

'Please, Mrs Blackstone,' said Mr Crain, as Emma started to rise. 'If you'll let me steal a little of your tea, that's all I need. What on earth,' he added after a moment, 'is the Empress of Babylon doing in Rome?'

Emma rolled her eyes. 'Time traveling, like that gentleman in Mr Wells's novel! I keep telling Mr Pugh that there *was* no Empress of Babylon during Nero's reign! Babylon was in ruins by that time – and Nero had a perfectly good Sinful Empress to persecute Christians.'

'Really?' The old man cocked his head. 'Are you sure? Because it makes much more sense, that the Empress of Babylon would have turned the Romans against Christianity. Why, John the Evangelist even said so, in *Revelation*. The Romans were such a sensible and virtuous civilization, I've always wondered why they persecuted the Christians in the first place.'

He had clearly never heard of the Emperor Caligula. Emma was still struggling to find a response that was both tactful and accurate when he added, 'I will take your word for it, though. Kitty tells me that you studied "all those ancient times" you went to Oxford, she says?'

'I did.' Emma smiled. 'I was up at Somerville College during the War. My father taught Classics at New College. His specialty was Etruscan inscriptions, though. He was really more of an archeologist than a historian. From the age of ten I was drafted to be his assistant. My mother kept telling him it was no occupation for a young lady.'

The lights went down; Madge's voice boomed from the direction of the set. *And what would Madge's mother*, Emma reflected, *have to say about HER occupation . . .?*

'And I suppose,' sighed Mr Crain, 'that had you been a boy, your mother would have been ecstatic to see you following in your father's footsteps.'

Emma turned her head quickly at the note of sadness in the old man's voice, and remembered things Kitty had told her about Crain's son Timothy. *An absolute STICK, darling! Ambrose tells me he lives with his mother on Long Island and never goes ANYWHERE but his office in the city. He's never even been out of NEW YORK! All he THINKS about is staying in his office and making money!*

Was that the family that would disown Mr Crain for donning Roman guise to stand in the back of a cinematic crowd?

'*LIGHTS! CAMERA!*'

The musicians plunged into the *Habanera* from *Carmen*. Ken Elmore – Elmore Perkins, at his baptism in Bismarck, North Dakota – glistening like his stand-in, with cocoa butter and just as skimpily semi-draped, lunged against his chains and bared his teeth, as Scotty and Ginny retreated beyond the camera line and lit cigarettes.

'*ACTION!!!*'

The Temptress of Babylon, sinuous as a cobra and beautiful as the night, appeared in the doorway of the dungeon cell.

Mr Crain heaved a sigh of beatific ecstasy.

'Get the fuck out of my dungeon, bitch!' shouted the saintly Christian Demetrius, wrenching at his bonds, and Valerna raised her hands like claws.

'Fool!' she cried. 'I'm going to screw you senseless!'

The title cards for this interchange, Emma recalled, would read: *Begone, harlot!* And *Yield to the embraces of the Goddess of Love!*

One can only hope there are no lip-readers in the audience . . .

The millionaire chuckled softly, and murmured, 'Oh, dear, oh dear oh dear . . .'

'Mr Crain,' murmured Emma, below the dark gleam of the music. 'Mr Rokatansky told me that you offered last night to help us. I think . . . I know it sounds melodramatic, but I think there's something going on with this murder, something beyond what meets the eye.'

He looked surprised. 'I thought it was bootleggers. All the newspapers – and the film magazines – say that Mr Festraw was mixed up with gangsters.'

'I know,' said Emma. 'And yet there's something . . . I may be completely wrong. But there's something about the affair that doesn't . . . doesn't *smell* right to me. It sounds silly—'

'Not silly at all, m'am.' He set down his mug of tea. 'I've had the same experience with financial transactions. Everything my broker laid out on paper looked perfectly above-board and profitable, and yet . . . it's as if little alarm bells were ringing in the distance. Or like the smell of smoke when you're dropping off to sleep.'

Emma said, very quietly, 'Yes.'

'What would you like me to do?'

'Do you know of anyone in New York – or know how we might find someone in New York – who could be trusted to find out about Mr Festraw there? Find out who this Stanislas Markham is, who paid for Mr Festraw to come out to Los Angeles? And anything else about Mr Festraw that it would help us to know?'

This had been Zal's suggestion. Frank Pugh had studio money – as indeed did Kitty – but there was far greater likelihood (said Zal) of Pugh being mixed up in this than old Mr Crain.

'I'll put in a call to our New York offices tomorrow,' he said at once. 'I remember we hired . . . well, an investigator in New York a few years ago, when my son had . . . a little trouble with . . . with the consequences of falling into bad company.' A slight flush darkened his cheekbones and he looked aside, mortified.

Emma thought, *Good heavens!* Did the dull stick Timothy Crain step out a little wide with a showgirl after all? But the old man seemed so disturbed that she only said, 'Thank you. That is most good of you.'

At nearly eleven, Kitty came tripping over from the dungeon between takes to eat another wonton ('Sweets for the sweet,' murmured Mr Crain, a malicious twinkle in his eyes) and kiss her elderly inamorato goodbye. 'I'm sure your Mr Pugh will be along any moment,' Mr Crain said, 'and is bound to frown on outsiders watching the magic of Hollywood taking place.'

Which was, Emma thought, a tactful way of putting it.

'Dreadful as it would be for members of my board to glimpse me in Roman armor at the back of a cinema film, it would be a thousand times worse for tomorrow's headlines to read, "Corporation President Ejected from Film Studio" . . .'

'Darling, he never would!' cried Kitty. 'You're a stockholder! But you're right – Frank is *so* jealous . . .'

She spoke in her film-vamp voice – as if it were nothing to her, to have men quarreling over her like a latter-day Ninon de l'Enclos – but Emma reflected that now was *not* the time for her to lose the support of her studio. She also was aware of a twinge of uneasiness, seeing Darlene Golden – who was not a part of this scene at all – still lingering in the shadows of the garden set beyond the open rear doors, watching Kitty's visitor with narrowed eyes. And indeed, not ten minutes after Mr Crain took his leave (and Emma prudently disposed of his mug back on the trestle tables at the front of the stage) Frank Pugh entered, looking tired and crumpled. Kitty abandoned the saintly Demetrius mid-embrace, and rushed to the producer's side to clasp his hands, press her forehead (being very careful not to disarrange her make-up) against his massive shoulder, and gaze up with what looked like genuine worship in her eyes.

He bent his head over hers, gathered her small hands against his breast. Madge looked as if she might have said something, but didn't.

Darlene looked as if she might have spit blood . . . but didn't.

'*Darling,*' Kitty cooed a moment later, hurrying back to

Emma, 'Frank and I are going to go have a little bite at the Café Montmartre when we're done here – and Madge says we have only one or two more takes left . . . and then we'll be going on to Peggy's. She's having a little get-together, and I think' – she lowered her voice conspiratorially – 'Frank wants to pump her about Lou Jesperson's new projects at Enterprise. Would you be an *angel* and take my little beloveds home?' She crouched gracefully to gather the eagerly wriggling Chang Ming into her arms. The other two Pekes stood on their hind-legs, forepaws on her knees and back, licking their own noses with excited delight. 'And could you get Zal to drive my car? He can take a cab home, charged to the studio account . . . Zal, *darling* . . .'

She scurried to the cameraman's side.

Thus Emma packed up the camp chairs, the magazine bin, folded up the make-up table and neatly consolidated the un-eaten remains of the feast into two containers, and by the time she'd given the Pekes a final constitutional outside, the last few takes had been taken, and Zal brought Kitty's big yellow Packard around to the door of Stage One.

Emma sank into the soft leather of the upholstery as the big car purred along Sunset Boulevard – stilled now in the deeps of the night – and turned up the darkness of the Cahuenga Pass. Stars sprinkled the sky, brighter as they wound up into the hills; the white shapes of pseudo-Spanish houses glimmered among fan-palms, and a coyote trotted across the road. In the back seat, the Pekes snored in their boxes.

Emma's hand stole into the pocket of her cardigan. For thirty-six hours, she had been dragged like Alice through the looking-glass country – doing all the running she could, just to stay in the same place – and aside from the sleep she'd snatched when they'd finally gotten home last night, had been preoccupied with rewriting scenes twenty to twenty-four in one of her pile of school copybooks. Added to this had been the chore of getting Kitty to where she needed to be and keeping track of the dogs and trying to sort out what it was about this whole business of the murder that troubled her so deeply . . .

But not for a moment had Aunt Estelle's letter been completely gone from her mind.

She was exhausted now, but in the quiet of the car – Zal, blessedly, seemed to sense that stillness was what she craved – she went back over the words.

Over the memories.

The Myrtles . . . *How will I ever live close enough to walk to The Myrtles, without feeling grief whenever I turn down Holywell Street?*

Her parents' grave, in the Wolvercote Cemetery. Miles asleep for eternity beside them. *It will be good to be able to visit. To remember without pain . . . or with much less pain . . .*

She didn't know where Jim was buried. The War Department had written her a letter – it was one of the many things that hadn't been in that single small suitcase that somebody had saved for her when they'd cleared out the house. It didn't matter, really, since the letter had contained no information either. Only the date, and the information that his effects would be mailed to her, which they hadn't been.

If I return to Oxford I'll be able to look up my old friends again. Did Anne Littleton ever return from the Front? Is Professor Etheridge still lecturing at Sommerville? So many people had simply disappeared from her life, in the wake of the War and the epidemic. Letters returned unanswered. *No Longer Here*, printed on the envelopes. As it had been, she knew, on the letters that had arrived at The Myrtles for her . . .

She closed her eyes. *I'll be able to look them up again . . .*

Somewhere in the hills to the west, along Wedgewood Avenue, Peggy Donovan's preposterous castellated mansion was lit up like a Christmas tree, her guests whooping and shrieking with laughter around her swimming pool . . . her *two* swimming pools . . . while a fortune teller in an Arabian tent in the rear of the property read peoples' palms. Just the thought of the noise made Emma shudder. *What am I doing here?*

And Zal's elbow brushed the side of her arm, accidentally and very lightly, as he turned the wheel and the big car swayed its way slowly down the steep drive. The dell at the bottom of the drive, below the road, was a well of indigo shadow, and on the opposite hillside Kitty's Moorish fantasy of a house seemed to glimmer in the moonlight. Opening her eyes, Emma saw the star-threaded outline of Zal Rokatansky's face, the glint of reflection in his glasses. After a day of sweating at the studio he still smelled, very faintly, of soap and bay rum. He turned the car around the big eucalyptus tree in the drive, stopped before the fancy tiled steps up to the porch. Getting out, he took Chang Ming's box and that of Black Jasmine. Emma withdrew Buttercreme's, and followed him up the steps. The porch light had been switched off, probably, she guessed, by the gardener's wife, a tiny, bent Chinese woman who watched every penny spent in the household, as if they were paupers.

Can I leave Zal?

And can I find my house key . . .?

In their boxes, Chang Ming and Black Jasmine both jolted suddenly, and set up a salvo of barking.

Emma stopped on the porch steps in the moonlight, looking up. Behind her, Zal set down the boxes he carried, called out, 'Who's there?'

Emma turned to retreat as a shadow moved in the porch, and she saw another shadow emerge from the tangle of rhododendron that grew around the tall foundation of the house. A man's dark shape reached the bottom step in two strides and a man's deep voice commanded, 'Don't try it,' as Zal moved. To flee? To fight?

In the same moment the man from the porch reached her and caught her arm in a frighteningly powerful grip. The two male Pekes in their boxes were yapping furiously, challenging, like enraged lions, and she saw that both men had guns.

NINE

Another voice said, from the black abyss of the porch, 'There's nuthin' to be afraid of, Miss. Mr Cornero just wants to have a few words with you.' And then: 'Shut them mutts up, will you, Rico?'

Emma said, in a voice that astonished her by its calm, 'They're only doing their jobs – as I'm sure you are as well.'

This second man emerged from the shadows and descended the steps to her, even as another – also brandishing a pistol – joined the one who stood next to Zal.

'May I get my house key?' she continued. 'I promise you I don't have a weapon in my handbag.'

And the man next to her said, 'Crap, it's the secretary. Where's Miss de la Rose?'

'Having a late dinner at the Club Montmartre,' said Emma. 'Can we all go inside? Or at least switch on the porch light? Yes, I'm Mrs Blackstone, Miss de la Rose's secretary . . .'

A third man came down the steps, held out a gloved hand politely to her. His accent was pure radio-hoodlum, but his voice was pleasant. 'I'm sorry we have to bother you this way, Mrs Blackstone, but there's a couple things we need to get straightened out, and you can't be too careful in my business.'

After shaking her hand he descended another two steps to offer his hand to Zal. 'Tony Cornero,' he introduced himself.

'Zal Rokatansky. I take it this is in connection with Rex Festraw?'

The first hoodlum having released her arm, Emma set Buttercreme's carry-box down on the step, located her house keys by touch in the dark of her handbag. 'Could you get that box for me, please?' *No reason a gun-toting gangster can't make himself useful . . .*

Mother would FAINT . . .

She unlocked the door, switched on the lights in the living room ('Put that bulb back in the porch light, Rico,' commanded Cornero over his shoulder), and said, 'Thank you,' as the gunman set the little dog's box down near the door. Zal entered, flanked by Cornero and his thugs and carrying the other two dogs.

'Hey, pooch.' Cornero bent to peer through the little wicker window at Chang Ming. 'They bite?'

'They couldn't do you any harm if they did,' pointed out Zal, and the bootlegger laughed.

'Like hell they couldn't! Worst bite I ever got in my life was from that little dustmop that belonged to my stepfather's landlady in North Beach. *Che lupa*, what a bitch! I had to get like five stitches on my arm!'

Tony the Hat, a little to Emma's surprise, turned out to be a year or two younger than herself – not yet twenty-five, she guessed – a good-looking young man of medium height with intelligent dark eyes and a pleasant manner. He turned to his men and said, 'I think we're OK here, boys,' and the men obediently trooped out onto the porch. Emma indicated one of the sleek, black-and-chrome chairs, and seated herself on the couch, with Zal, quiet but wary, at her side.

'I am glad to make your acquaintance, Mr Cornero,' she said. 'All the way back from downtown this afternoon I was cudgeling my brains, to come up with some way of asking you a few questions about Mr Festraw, so this all works out very nicely – I hope. You didn't . . . Are Mr Shang – the gardener – and his wife all right? They're down in the cottage—'

'Oh, yeah, yeah!' The bootlegger raised both hands with a slight pushing gesture, palms out, as if to show them clean of innocent blood. 'One of my boys is down there with them, that's all. Just to make sure they don't get excited and phone the cops or anything. Not that I have any reason to worry about the law,' he added quickly. 'Just . . . people misinterpret things, you know?'

Being held at gunpoint would certainly lead one to jump to conclusions, Emma was careful not to say. And in fact from all she'd heard, Tony Cornero *didn't* have any need to fear the

law in Los Angeles. Instead she turned to Zal, said, 'Zal, could
I possibly trouble you to make some coffee? I'm sure it will
be all right.' That last was in reply to his look, not to any
words spoken.

'It will,' said Cornero. 'Really. And thank you, Mrs
Blackstone.' He touched the brim of his pale-ivory fedora
respectfully. 'I appreciate it. What makes you think I had
anything to do with Rex Festraw?' he added, with an appearance of innocence. 'I came here because, frankly, I was
disturbed by what the movie rags are saying, that I or my
brother Frank might have had something to do with the man's
death. We're businessmen, Mrs Blackstone. We're not gangsters. If movie stars go around murdering their ex-husbands,
that's one thing, but that kind of rumor and slander can be
very harmful.'

'Oh, quite,' agreed Emma. '*He that hath a bad name is half
hanged*, as the Scots say. But – please correct me if I'm wrong
– I understand that Mr Festraw did work for you last Friday,
and in fact may have . . . well, taken an unauthorized advance
on his salary.'

All the warmth vanished from his eyes, but he only tilted
his head a little. 'Who'd you hear that from? Do you mind
me asking?'

'An acquaintance of his,' she returned. 'Of course I have
no idea how true it is, and haven't spoken to anyone about it.
And I suspect the name she gave me – Elizabeth Bennet –
wasn't her own. But she did show me some quite impressive
pieces of jewelry that she said he'd bought her.' She folded
her hands composedly. 'Now, I'm not sure where the publicity
department of Foremost Productions – or the columnists who
write for *Screen Stories* and *Photo Play* – get their information, but they did seem to know that Mr Festraw was associated
with bootleggers in New York. They may simply have drawn
an inference that he would seek out similar business opportun-
ities in Los Angeles, to earn himself some extra money while
preparing to blackmail Miss de la Rose. The young lady I
spoke to did seem to be a fairly expensive proposition.'

The corner of Cornero's mouth tugged sidelong, and under
the sleek, expensive suiting, his shoulders relaxed. 'Rex

Festraw was small-time,' he said dismissively. 'The dough he stole from me – well, he heisted a motorboat with sixty cases of single-malt Scotch in it – that was penny-ante. Twenty-five hundred bucks, tops. What kind of a man would risk a rap for conspiracy to do murder for that kind of chicken feed?'

Emma's brow creased a little. 'That does seem an extremely modest amount. Now, there were Roman Emperors – Tiberius springs to mind – who would have had men cut up and fed to their pet eels, for quite trivial transgressions, simply because seeing it done had such a good effect on their other servants.'

'Roman Emperors had pet eels?'

'Oh, yes,' said Emma. 'Not pets, precisely, but eels were considered a delicacy, and the Emperors Tiberius and Caligula kept great pools of them, so they could have eel for dinner whenever they wanted.'

'Wouldn't that affect the taste of the meat?'

'I should think so,' agreed Emma. 'But I don't imagine either Tiberius or Caligula would much care. And of course,' she added, 'as Emperors of Rome, they could get away with that sort of lesson to their subordinates much more easily than someone like – what name did Miss Bennet mention? Joe Adonis? – could.'

'Yeah, but if you fed Rex Festraw to a bunch of eels,' grinned Cornero, 'they'd get so drunk they'd just float down to the bottom of the pond an' lay there. Same goes for anybody who ate the meat off 'em. Thank you,' he added, as Zal came in with two cups of coffee and one – to Emma's touched delight – of tea, on a tray.

'Who fed Rex Festraw to eels?' inquired Zal, but Emma noticed he kept a wary eye on Cornero and glanced swiftly around the room to make sure 'the boys' were all still back on the porch.

'The Emperor of Rome,' said the bootlegger with a laugh. 'That's a new one, I'll remember that. But I tell you honestly, Mrs Blackstone,' he said, 'I had nothing to do with Festraw buying it. Yeah, if he hadn't paid me the full price of that Glenfiddich I won't say he wouldn't have been sorry – and from what I've heard about him from the New York boys, I

don't think they'd have shed a lot of tears over him comin'
to grief. But the fact is, he wasn't one of my regular boys. I
put him in charge of drivin' a motorboat, not distribution or
set-up. Joe Adonis suggested Festraw might be useful for little
jobs, but I wouldn't put a new man in charge of anythin' worth
– well, worth runnin' any risks over.' He shrugged. 'Even the
Roman emperors would be smarter than that.'

'I suspect,' said Emma, 'that when anyone says "bootlegger", people find that a handy explanation.'

'They do. When all I'm really doin' is savin' a hundred an'
twenty million people from bein' poisoned by the homemade
stuff. By the way,' he added, reaching into his coat, 'if you'd
care for—'

'No, thank you.' Emma smiled.

'Kitty'll kill you,' warned Zal.

'Kitty has three dozen bottles of everything you could
name in the kitchen cupboards. And *none* of it homemade.'
She turned back to Cornero. 'But thank you very much for
the thought, all the same, Mr Cornero. Did Mr Festraw happen
to mention to you having some other job on hand? Another
source of income in Los Angeles?'

The young man pondered for a moment. He was little
more than a boy, Emma judged, and by his accent had immi-
grated from Italy, but his well-fitting brown suit and subdued
silk tie were the garments of a very wealthy man. Evidently
saving the population of the United States from its own
bathtub gin was an extremely profitable undertaking. The
diamond on his pinkie-ring was small enough to be real but
large enough to have cost the price of a new car – six months
with Kitty had made Emma something of a connoisseur of
diamonds. When he took off his gloves to handle the coffee
cup, she noticed that his hands were manicured. This was a
man – like Colt Madison – who took his personal appearance
seriously.

'To hear Festraw tell it,' he said at last, 'he needed the job
somethin' bad. But he was stayin' at the Winterdon, which
ain't no flophouse. An' one of my boys said he'd seen Festraw
at the Bel Giardino – one of my nightclubs – buyin' drinks
for a dame who was makin' like a napkin in his lap. This was

Sunday night, so he was either spendin' what he'd got sellin' my liquor under the table, or he had some other source of dough, or both. I was reservin' judgment til Friday, when he was supposed to hand me the delivery money for the shipment.'

'And he didn't tell you how he happened to be staying at the Winterdon?'

Cornero shook his head. 'I thought that sounded a little screwy at the time, but it wasn't my business. If somethin' had happened and I hadn't got my dough Friday, then maybe I'd have asked some questions.'

'Were you keeping an eye on him?' Zal made a gesture to lift the coffee pot again, to which the bootlegger shook his head with a motion of thanks.

'Not really, though if he'd taken a powder my boys would have been able to find out where in a coupla hours. You know how it is. Everybody knows somebody, all over town. He wouldn't't'a been hard to find.'

Emma considered the matter. 'Do you know anyone – or know *of* anyone – named Stanislas Markham? I think he's in New York.'

'Yeah,' said Cornero at once. 'Stan Markham – Stan the Mark. He's sort of medium smalltime in Queens. He's got a club – the Four Queens – but he does all kinds of stuff: launders a little money, runs crap games, maybe arranges shipments in from Canada for Luciano. Nice guy. Stays out of trouble and keeps his nose clean.'

'According to the clerk at the Winterdon, Mr Markham wired the money for Mr Festraw's room.'

'Makes sense,' agreed Cornero. 'If I was sendin' somebody someplace on a job, I'd have Stan make arrangements for me. What I can't get is who'd do that for Festraw? I mean, he may know Adonis and Luciano to recommend him, but he's not *connected* connected. He's not in with any of the big *pezzo-novantes* that I've ever heard of. Takin' a look at him, I wouldn't't'a put him as worth the buck-fifty a night it cost to put him up at the Winterdon. So what gives?'

'I don't know,' returned Emma. 'But something obviously does. Would this Mr Markham happen to know any forgers?'

'Oh, yeah! Stan can get you set up with anybody on the East Coast. You send him the stationery, and a sample of your mark's fist, he'll get you turned around in a week. That's what they tell me, anyway.' He looked a little self-conscious at having this knowledge.

Emma reflected briefly on the number of people who came and went through the studio gates every day – from delivery boys to agents to Thelma Turnbit slipping dollar bills to Floyd – and the fact that almost nobody locked the doors of their dressing rooms. 'And would you by chance have heard of anyone else who'd have reason to kill Mr Festraw? Someone who might have thought that having Miss de la Rose accused of the crime might distract everyone's attention from any other motive?'

She was aware of Zal watching the younger man's face as Cornero turned the question over in his mind. He didn't look shifty, she thought. But then, it was part of his job not to.

At length he shook his head. 'I ain't heard nuthin',' he said. 'And I think my own boys would have told me, if he'd been dealin' with anybody else in town.'

'I should think so, too,' agreed Emma. 'Thank you. And taking such pains to cover the murder doesn't really make sense, for someone as . . . as *insignificant* as Mr Festraw. It isn't as if he were wealthy or famous, or that the police would really care who killed him, you know. I'll speak to Mr Fishbein about soft-pedaling any innuendos that Mr Festraw might have been shot by bootleggers. Quite honestly,' she added, 'if you were trying to kill Mr Festraw yourself, I think you'd do a much better job of it.'

'You're tellin' me!' he agreed, and then added, 'If I were the kind of person who'd do a terrible thing like that, which I'm not.'

'No, of course not. And if the murder was an attempt to cause trouble for Miss de la Rose, it was so clumsily done that again, I can't imagine any halfway intelligent criminal would be behind it.'

'Well, you got some dumb palookas in the business,' said Cornero. 'And I'll keep my ear out for anything I might hear. But anybody who's running any kind of racket in this town

knows enough to be careful around the studios. I'm not sayin'
there aren't producers an' stars mixed up with some shady
characters, but this . . . I think you're right, m'am. This just
feels . . . screwy. An' as far as I know, Camille de la Rose
isn't involved with anything or anybody sketchy – not the way
some of 'em are. I'll let you know if I hear anything.'

'And I'll do for you what I can,' promised Emma, rising.
'Though I doubt I'll be able to do anything about the fan
magazines . . .'

'Oh, hell, nobody can do anythin' about them broads.
Ladies,' he corrected himself, standing up also and picking up
his hat. 'Thanks for the coffee, m'am. An' if you're ever down
in Santa Monica, stop by the Bel Giardino an' tell 'em I said
to give you an' Mr Rokatansky here drinks on the house.'

As he went out onto the porch, Emma heard him say, 'We're
good, Rico. Go down let the gardener an' his wife outta that
closet.'

'You all right?' asked Zal, some time later, after they had
descended to the rear yard – which lay further around the
slope of the hill – and made sure that the ancient Mr Shang
and his tiny, ancient wife had been no worse than frightened
when two of Cornero's men had imprisoned them in a closet.
The phoneline, Emma had discovered the moment the bootleggers' car had disappeared onto Ivarene Street, had been cut,
probably before she and Zal had even returned to the house
that evening.

When they climbed the tall flight of wooden back-stairs to
the kitchen again she found that she was shaking, whether
from delayed fear or due to the fact that it was now three
o'clock in the morning, she wasn't certain.

'I think so.' She sank into one of the kitchen chairs, and
Zal poured her out what was left of the tea. Then he dumped
the contents of both cartons of Chinese food into a pan,
added a little water, and put it on the stove to heat. 'My
father used to tell me about having to pay protection money
to bands of banditti in the Apennines . . . He'd make a funny
story of it, but I think he wanted to make sure that when I
did go, I wouldn't wander away from camp, like those silly

girls in novels are always doing. My mother was horrified, of course.'

'I'd be, if you were my daughter.' His eyes met hers, smiling.

'He kept saying he'd teach me to shoot before we went. But then he'd get distracted by some new findings somebody had published, or an eighth-century palimpsest that had part of the *Aeneid* written on it, and I'd be back in the study cataloging variations of letter shape and usage . . .' She shook her head quickly.

'No wonder Hollywood history drives you nuts.' He carried two plates over to the table. 'Do you miss it?'

'I . . . I do.' She thought she'd be far too upset by the night's events to eat, but found that after the first mouthful of rice and chow mein that she not only felt much better, but was ravenous. 'Sometimes I felt like the Lady of Shalott, locked up in a tower weaving tapestries of the tales of other peoples' lives, that she could see only in a mirror . . .' She shook her head. 'But it was my life. And I was good at it. And I really couldn't imagine doing anything else, until I met Jim.'

It felt strange to pronounce Jim's name to him, as if Jim were still alive somewhere, still married to her. She heard her voice stammer a little on the name, and for an instant it was as if he had just left the room.

As if he'd just gotten on the boat-train to Dover, to go back to his unit in France.

She'd stood on the platform for a quarter of an hour after the train was gone, she remembered. As if somehow, if she waited long enough, the train would come back and Jim would hop down from its doorway and say, 'Hey, it was all a mistake . . .!'

As if everything that had happened since was all a mistake . . .

The night's silence deepened outside, and the ticking of the kitchen clock seemed suddenly loud. Wherever Kitty was – and the party was undoubtedly still going on at Peggy Donovan's – she wasn't going to be home that night. Emma glanced at the clock as Zal poured himself the last of the cold, over-brewed coffee and downed it. Scene seventy-eight was shooting tomorrow and he had to be on the set at seven . . .

The thought of the terrible silence in the house when he left made her shiver, and Zal asked quietly, 'Would you like me to stay?'

She said, 'I know they're not coming back.'

'Oh, I know that, too. But that's not what I asked.'

Softly, she said, 'Yes. Please.'

TEN

Emma woke late, after a dream that she'd had often before. When she was twelve, her father had told her that back in the first century AD, the Roman Emperor Claudius had rounded up the last of the native Etruscans from the Italian hills and had written an Etruscan–Latin dictionary. Her father had been fond of cursing the Christian monks and barbarian chieftains who had been responsible for the disappearance of this invaluable volume during the Dark Ages, and thereafter Emma had dreamed periodically of finding the book, bound and strapped in iron and gold, with *Etruscis Latine Lexicon Manuale – Scriptus a Tiberius Claudius Nero Germanicus* written on the cover. (Emma frequently dreamed in Latin. Occasionally she dreamed in what she knew to be Etruscan, which she, unlike any scholar in the waking world, spoke perfectly in her dreams.)

And there was always a moment before actual waking, when she dreamed she awoke, lying in her bed, with the book clasped in her arms. Delight would fill her like warm sunlight (*Father will be so pleased!*) . . .

And then she'd waken 'for real', as the children said, and the book would be gone.

Zal had left her a note on her night-table, and, she discovered when she descended to the kitchen in her bathrobe, had fed the dogs and filled the kettle for tea. Conscientiously, Emma washed, dressed, boiled an egg for breakfast, and walked down the hill to Franklin Avenue, to make a call to the telephone company to have the line repaired. A further call to the studio established that Kitty was there and shooting scene sixty-three. She left one message with Vinnie begging Kitty to excuse her absence that day, and another to Zal, saying only, *Thank you*. No sense in saying more, for the edification and amusement of everyone in the studio. Kitty had not been exaggerating when she'd complained of studio gossip.

Emma did wonder briefly how anyone could consummate a romantic tryst on the catwalks above the lights in Stage Three – but if anyone could do it, Kitty could.

The men from the telephone company did not arrive until four. Emma spent a meditative day brushing the dogs, balancing Kitty's check-book, paying the bills and excising the fortune teller from scenes twenty through twenty-four (and from scene seventy-nine, where he made a reappearance among the flames of burning Rome to pronounce the doom of Babylon).

And reading Aunt Estelle's letter.

Thinking about Oxford.

Thinking about home.

At five, when the telephone repairman departed – sped on his way by the indignant yapping of the Pekes – Emma made herself another cup of tea, consulted the *Times*, then switched on the kitchen radio, to hear what the Pettingers had to say about the events of Wednesday afternoon.

She was not disappointed. Bushrod Pettinger had a rather nasal, but very powerful, voice, and ringingly denounced Hollywood and all its works. 'Abraham warned his brother Lot, "Do not pitch your tents towards Sodom!".' Emma wondered how many of Mr Pettinger's listeners were sufficiently familiar with the Book of Genesis to know that Lot was Abraham's nephew, not his brother. Or did they care? 'Abraham warned his brother that if he so much as dwelled near the Cities of the Plain, great evil would befall him, and he would stand in danger not only of his life, but of his very soul!'

Between regular attendance at Sunday school, and Oxford lectures about ancient Mesopotamia, Emma had no recollection of the Patriarch saying a word to his nephew about the spiritual ramifications of real estate in one district over another. She wondered – albeit for only the minutest fraction of a moment – whether Kitty had such a thing as a Bible in her house, to check.

'And so it was then,' intoned Miss Pettinger, who had a surprisingly beautiful contralto even over the airwaves, 'and so it is today! Heed the warning, I beg you, my brothers and sisters in Christ! Turn your face away from the painted lures of the Devil, the garish evil that rolls out of every motion-picture palace and nickelodeon! Walk away from those photoplays about harlots and hooligans and cry with Jesus, "Get thee behind me, Satan!".'

'*Nickelodeon?*' Like a gorgeous dragonfly in the frock of changeable eggplant and green that she'd had on yesterday, Kitty appeared in the kitchen door from the rear yard. 'Are there even nickelodeons *around* anymore? Oh, my little sweet-nesses!' She crouched, to receive the ecstatic greetings of her furry pets, and an instant later looked up and cried, 'Oh, darling, are you all right? Zal told me – *NO*, Jazz! *Down*, Chang . . . Zal told me what happened last night – and the Shangs, just now when I put the car away. How *awful!*' She stood, and impulsively caught Emma in a hug. 'I'm *so* sorry!'

'There's no need for you to be sorry,' pointed out Emma. 'It had nothing to do with you.'

'Oh, but darling, it *did*! If it hadn't been for me you wouldn't even *be* in California! Were you terrified? I've met Tony Cornero at his club and he really wouldn't hurt a fly – well, not someone who wasn't another gangster, anyway . . .'

Reflecting on the other things that bootleggers – like Taffy in the prop warehouse – were likely to be selling, not to speak of the darker end of the business of prostitution, Emma would not have gone so far as to say that. 'Oddly enough, I wasn't really afraid,' she admitted. 'Not until they'd all left. Then I . . . I rather went to pieces for a bit . . .'

'The *exact* same thing happened to me when Ruggy Brevoort – or was it Clayton, before we got married? – crashed his roadster on the Jones Beach Parkway at two o'clock in the morning. The car rolled completely over and it's a miracle neither of us was killed, or even hurt, except that I got motor oil leaked onto my pastel silk. I must have chewed him out for fifteen minutes and then we had to hitch-hike back to his place, and I didn't say a word to him . . . Oh, no, it was Bert Englemeier! Because he had this marvelous house at Oyster Bay . . . But once I'd locked him out of my bedroom I just collapsed.'

She took Emma's hand in hers. 'Are you all right?' she asked, in another tone. Her voice was the voice of a friend, and the velvet-brown eyes, looking up into Emma's, were filled with concern, a friend's eyes.

Emma said, quietly, 'I'm fine.'

'You're sure?'

She smiled, and nodded. 'I'm sure.'

'Zal told me you promised to get me to talk to Fishy about laying off the bootlegger angle with the fan magazines, and I made Fishy promise that he would. And it took me for*ever* to catch him, because that *imbecile* Dirk kept screwing up his sword fight with Elmore, and Madge had us do *thirty-five takes*, because Dirk didn't want it to look like Elmore was winning—'

Emma switched off the radio. 'I hope he did lose in the end, or else I'm going to have to rewrite the last six scenes of the film, and I don't think Mr Pugh will be very happy about that.'

'Darling, he'll have a *stroke!*' She'd turned away and was fishing through the icebox, and emerged a moment later, with a scrap of chicken from the little dish of it that Emma had cooked up for the Pekes' dinners for the next few days. 'He was acting like an absolute *bear* all day, *glaring* at me as if I'd done something wrong at Peggy's party – which I *didn't!* I just *know* that witch Darlene has been telling him all sorts of horrible things . . . Oh, there's Mrs Shang!'

The rear stairs down to the yard below creaked slightly under the old lady's barely ninety pounds.

'Would you mind having dinner a little early, darling? They were still filming Nicky's scenes when I left and I'm *crushed* with exhaustion.' She dove into the icebox again and reemerged with the small dish of half-melted ice-chips that Emma had hacked from the main block earlier that afternoon. 'Oh, thank you for doing this! You're marvelous!' And she clattered up the steps to the dining room, the diamonds on her shoe-heels flashing. Emma picked a lime out of the basket on the counter, smiled a greeting to Mrs Shang, and followed. Kitty was already pouring gin into the shaker.

'What did you do at Peggy's?'

'*Nothing*, darling!' Kitty sought for something – probably the soda water – in the depths of the cabinet. 'I swear it, *nothing*! But that *nasty* old trout Prudence Pettinger – what on *Earth* were you doing listening to her anyway? – had the *nerve* to turn up at Enterprise Pictures today to complain about Peggy's party! Peggy told me. *Honestly*, it isn't like the Pettingers *live* in that neighborhood or anything! Myself, I think it was a little tacky of Peggy to tip off the newspapers about it, but we were only on the pavement for about ten minutes, so it couldn't really have hurt the horses' feet, and there's almost no traffic on Wedgewood Avenue at that hour, and you yourself told me only the other day that people in Ancient Greece rode horses not wearing any clothes all the time. Of course if you fell off you'd get a *heinous* scrape, but Peggy *did* warn her guests, and it was early enough in the evening that they couldn't have been *that* drunk . . .'

'Newspapers?'

Kitty dismissed the word with a breezy wave, but Emma thought she smiled, just the tiniest bit. 'Well, that's what I *hear*. And the Pettingers turned up outside the gate, positively *fulminating* fire and brimstone . . . and of course they're just *furious* about Gloria Swanson waltzing into the Montmartre last night with a cheetah on a leash and that *insanely* handsome cowboy from Metro . . .' She added soda water, and took a silver knife from the drawer – Emma was still amazed by the casual abundance of citrus fruit in California, limes and lemons and oranges as common as crab apples back home. 'I don't see why they blame *me* for it.'

'Do they?'

'Of course they do, darling!' Abandoning the lime, Kitty darted to the basket of magazines beside the telephone niche, and among the Chinese newspapers favored by the Shangs (and the *LA Opinion* that Dominga brought in on her cleaning days), found that morning's *Examiner*. 'Didn't you read the letter they wrote? Accusing me of – Oh, here it is! "Leading the virgin daughters of America into unspeakable sin . . ."' She unfolded the paper to the proper page. 'Though they don't seem to have any problem speaking about it. Fishy is absolutely over the *moon* with delight . . .'

'Delight?'

'Oh, *completely* delight, darling!' She returned to her

cocktail, her great dark eyes sparkling. After the day's shooting she had removed her camera make-up and repainted her face for the car-ride home, but under it, Emma could see the marks of fatigue. She wondered if her sister-in-law had slept at all last night (and if so, where?) – or if she had followed her own oft-spoken dictum, *Well, it's easier to STAY up than to GET up* . . . 'Everybody in the *country* knows they're only doing those crazy things to look as unspeakable and abandoned as I am. Fishy says, you can't buy publicity like that!'

She sipped the gin with visible ecstasy. 'Darlene can say what she likes about coke, darling, but it's gin for my money – and you're quite right,' she added. 'Dope *is* making Darlene's skin look coarse – you can see it in the dailies! I'm *so* glad you warned me what it was doing to my face. She's *such* an imbecile! Would you like some of this, darling?'

Emma refrained from mentioning Kitty's own consumption, up until a few months ago, of the too-common Hollywood 'pick-me-up', and said simply, 'Yes, please.' It had taken a co-ordinated effort between herself, Zal, and Mr Volmort in the make-up department to convince her sister-in-law that such things as cocaine and opium cigarettes were rendering her ugly and making her look thirty-five instead of 'twenty-four' . . . Kitty's colossal vanity had done the rest. (*'And honestly, dear, those cigarettes gave me SUCH a headache . . .'*) She wished she could similarly wean her from alcohol *but*, she told herself, *first things first* . . .

As Emma had pointed out last night, the contents of Kitty's liquor cabinet were the finest products of England and Canada – and had quite possibly been brought ashore by Mr Cornero himself. And whatever else could be said about her, Kitty was a superb bartender.

And then, when the time was right to start working on Kitty to cut down her drinking, Emma reflected, she, Emma, might well be back in Oxford. Walking across Magdalen Bridge on a misty autumn morning with her arms full of books. Saying to . . . to whom? Saying to a friend, to someone . . . *Oh, I lived in Hollywood for six months* . . .

Saying to friends a year, two years, ten years in the future (*Ten YEARS? 1934?*), *I used to live in Hollywood* . . .

With a laugh . . .

Did I ever tell you about the time we got held up by boot-leggers . . .?

The thought of Zal, kissing her last night in the kitchen. *Would you like me to stay?* A small, sharp blade turned a little in her heart.

The warmth of his arms around her. The solid strength of his shoulder under her cheek.

She closed a door on the memory, found again the letter from Bushrod Pettinger to the editor of the *Examiner*. Evidently – she read further down the column of Biblical brimstone – Miss Swanson and Miss Donovan weren't the only two actresses out to prove that they had more of 'It' than a gorgeous *femme fatale* accused of a mysterious murder. Last night while Peggy had been doing her impersonation of Lady Godiva on Wedgewood Avenue, Pola Negri had taken care to be seen dancing the tango with Rudolph Valentino at the Townhouse Club in a dress that 'would have brought a blush to the cheek of Salomé,' as Mr Pettinger had it, and earrings that had cost $950. The earrings worn by Gloria Swanson at the Café Montmartre – with the aforesaid riding extra and cheetah (which had thrown up a hairball onto the feet of the *maitre d'*) had cost $1750, and immediately after Peggy Donovan's bareback riding party, Clara Bow had challenged all comers to an auto race along Sunset Boulevard in the small hours of the morning.

This, fumed Mr Pettinger, was what came of encouraging celluloid wantons in extravagant misbehavior, and what would come of it, with such horrors glamorized before the eyes of the pure young girls of America, he wept to think.

'I wonder if I can get Ambrose to buy me that pair of diamond earrings I saw at Van Cleef and Arpel's last week,' mused Kitty, 'that cost two thousand seven hundred, for me to wear at the hearing?'

Zal telephoned her, just before eight – still at the studio, he said – to make sure all was well ('Other than the Pettingers preparing to launch a Holy War against us?'). It was good, only to hear his voice. But sleeping that night, Emma dreamed of Oxford. Oxford before the War, when she'd glide like a bird on her bicycle along Longwall Street, to The Misses Gibbs' Select Academy where she had been a day pupil, or to Mrs Willis's out along the Botley Road for her piano lessons. Walking with her mother early in the cool of May morning, to hear the choir singing in the Magdalen Tower. Seeing the undergraduates who looked so grown-up in their gowns when she was sixteen, that heartbreakingly beautiful summer before the War. Who looked so terribly young three years later, when she'd drive the ambulances from the train station to bring the wounded to hospital at Bicester. Sometimes, on warm nights in Michaelmas term, she had heard them strolling, late, along the Parks Road, singing. Those beautiful tenors and baritones, harmonizing in the dark.

In her dream she crossed the Magdalen Bridge, and quickened her step along Longwall Street. She thought, *I've missed them so. It will be good to see them again: Mother, Papa, Miles.* She had two of her father's books under her arm, and knew she'd taken them along to read when she'd been . . . wherever she'd been. Macaulay's *The Lays of Ancient Rome*, and a pocket copy of *Much Ado About Nothing*, always entertaining for a train ride . . . Her father would have acquired a catalog of the newest finds at the necropolis at Arrentium, he'd need help codifying the dates . . .

She glimpsed Miles, walking ahead of her. Miles jaunty and healthy, half-turning as if he'd wait for her, as he'd done ever since they were children, to go up the steps together.

But the house wasn't there. The place where it had stood on Holywell Street was only a thicket of trees, a tangle of overgrown rose bushes: albas, her mother's favorite, with petals fluffy as the skirts of Spanish dancers. The three shallow stone steps that had led up from the street to the door ended in nothing.

Miles was gone.

Emma cried, 'What happened?' and the effort to produce sound from her throat woke her.

For a moment she lay in the darkness, looking at the three tall, barely-seen rectangles of window opposite the foot of her bed and wondering, *What room am I in?*

The bow window of her bedroom at The Myrtles should have been there. The night-light (*That's not MY night-light . . . What happened to my little gold-glass night-light?*) showed her a low, square, boxy bureau, an unfamiliar chair.

And she remembered. Not one single thing from her bedroom had been saved, when they'd cleared out the house to sell. Someone from the hospital had gone in and gotten the clothes they'd thought she'd need, to go down to that dreary lodging in Headington, for the week she'd stayed, recuperating, before taking the train to Manchester and Mrs Pendergast's. Everything was gone.

All Father's notes had simply gone into the rubbish.

She'd never found out what had happened to Daphne, Mother's fat, white cat.

This wasn't the first time she'd waked like this, for one second puzzled that she wasn't in her own bedroom. It had happened every few weeks, during the horrible years she'd spent at Mrs Pendergast's.

It just felt like the first time.

It always felt like the first time.

It was Chang Ming barking.

Not the furious, defensive intruder-bark of last night, but the wary 'whuff' of suspicion.

Doggy toe-nails clattered in the hall outside her room. Black Jasmine gave a short yap as well, like a little quack.

Not enough to wake Kitty, Emma didn't think. After dinner her sister-in-law had had her usual round of telephone calls to Peggy Donovan ('*Did* I do anything really frightful last night, darling?'), Marie Prevost over at Warners (who was one of her main competitors for the title of the Silver Screen Goddess), and Blanche Sweet, one of the longtime reigning queens of Hollywood. But at nine fifteen Emma had come into Kitty's room and found her sleeping like a dead woman, the softly-complaining telephone under her nerveless hand.

It was now – she glanced at the clock on the nightstand – a quarter past one in the morning.

Headlights briefly swept Emma's window, then quickly died.

Cornero.

The glint of starlight on gun barrels leaped to her mind.

A deep voice saying, *Don't try it*. And then, *Where's Miss de la Rose?*

Emma swept her robe from the foot of her bed, wrapped it around her as she went to the window in the hall that looked out over the silly pseudo-balcony above the porch, and so down into the scrubby vale that was the front yard.

Kitty stood there, a darkly shimmering figure in the moonlight. From the shadows of the eucalyptus tree a man emerged, little more than a tall silhouette, and the white V-shaped gleam of a shirt-front. Dark hair, and the glisten of brilliantine – Emma thought, *Drat it!* as he approached, and Kitty, shaking back the dark cascade of her tousled hair, stretched out her arms to him.

Then movement at the top of the bank above them caught Emma's eye, and the drench of moonlight – only a day or two from full – showed her a man standing on the edge of the road, and the glint of something metal in his hands.

ELEVEN

Emma wrenched at the window-sash but the latch held fast. French doors opened from Kitty's room onto the balcony – she had almost reached them when she realized that the moonlight that shone so brightly on the tumble of sheets on the bed outlined a woman's hand and wrist. Hand and wrist and tousle of black curls among the pillow-lace.

She stood for a moment, then stepped close to the bed.

That was Kitty, all right. Sleeping like an innocent child, her other arm curved around Buttercreme, whose little round head rested in the hollow of her shoulder.

Quietly, Emma walked to the French doors, and looked out.

The dark-haired woman and the man in evening dress were still embracing, with a theatrical abandon that looked like progressing on to the honeymoon stage right there in the moonlight between the steep slope of the road-bank and the house.

It's Kitty's own house. Why fornicate in the front yard when there's a perfectly good bed . . .

The dress the dark-haired woman was wearing was the one Kitty had had on Wednesday night at the police station.

The one she got from the wardrobe department.

Which has at least three duplicates . . .

Ire smote her. Not anger or rage . . . simple vexation, as she understood what she was looking at.

OH!!!

She would have stamped her foot, had she not feared to wake Kitty – the genuine Kitty – sound asleep in her own bed . . .

Emma yanked the belt of her robe tight, ghosted back into her own room long enough to get her slippers, then ran lightly down the stairs, through the kitchen – catching up the house-keys from the counter and locking the back door behind her – and down the back steps. The inky shadow of the hill blanketed the driveway itself – concealing the rather seedy little